SNARL

SNARL

John Francis Pearring Jr.

Foreword by Timothy Fuller

Illustrated by Xander Redfern

RESOURCE *Publications* · Eugene, Oregon

SNARL

Resource Publications
An Imprint of Wipf and Stock Publishers
199 W. 8th Ave., Suite 3
Eugene, OR 97401

www.wipfandstock.com

PAPERBACK ISBN: 978-1-6667-4556-6
HARDCOVER ISBN: 978-1-6667-4557-3
EBOOK ISBN: 978-1-6667-4558-0

MAY 27, 2022 8:27 AM

To Joanne

Contents

FOREWORD

THE CREATION IS THE foundational miracle from which all else follows. God saw that it was good, and everything in it good without qualification. The inhabitants of Creation are all created—creatures—having been brought into being. They have beginnings and thus the possibility of endings. *Snarl* is an imaginative exploration of how, within whatever natural limits pertain to their kind, all creatures make sense of their situation. Human beings have an especially acute awareness of their situatedness. They are able thus to imagine becoming un-situated, of losing the marks of their identity even as they strive to retain them. They imagine what we call death.

Specifically, the story of Snarl the lion, and the other animals we meet here, suggests how, within their imaginative limits, the animals observe the possibilities of and threats to their persistence. The animals (lions, wolves, owls, coyotes, ravens, deer) do not extrapolate to the thought of the eternal, but the human imagination imagines it for them. In this sense the novelist is a creator imitating the divine act of creation which is what it means to be made in the image of God.

It is characteristic of the religious dimension of human existence to imagine what persists beyond, thus surmounting, death. It is imaginatively possible also for humans to wonder if something akin to their awareness of situatedness occurs in the other creatures as well. There are those who deny that possibility for animals as there are those who think it unimaginable that any of Creation's creatures cannot participate in the full range of Creation's possibilities. The question arises, "Can all of the creatures of Creation be redeemed?"

This story affirms that possibility by imagining that, if the Creation is God's handiwork nothing in it can depart from His jurisdiction, His intention that the Creation is good. At the same time, because all creatures given their limits must imagine what they only see imperfectly, their imaginations must ultimately depend on faith as the substance of what is not seen, the evidence of a possibility not yet, so far as they can see, fully realized. Imagining this possibility on behalf of the animals is the author's extension of his faith in what is not seen, to embrace all the other creatures. This is his affirmation of the Creation for all immersed within it who cannot, at least not yet, see the Creation directly and comprehensively as God knows it.

PROFESSOR TIMOTHY FULLER
April, 2022

Tim Fuller has a B.A. and M.A. from Kenyon College and a Ph.D. from Johns Hopkins University. He teaches in the Political Science department of Colorado College, since 1965, chairing the department from 1985 to 1991. He was Dean of the Faculty and College from 1992 to 1999 and served as Acting President from August 2001 to January 2002.

PREFACE

THOUGH TALK ABOUT DEATH and violence seem stark for our brittle hearts, the opposite is true. We're obsessed with the subject of life's suffering. I introduce animal circumstances in this novel to present a reasonable though difficult to confirm story about this problem we and animals share.

Our human experiences follow similar travails, as do animals. The paths we take hopefully lead to a better life. Judeo-Christian believers and those of the Islamic faiths visualize a good and holy next life juxtaposed against a damnable hell in eternity. Even non-believers know about the believers' story. Eternity's heaven and hell are well-known.

Believers say death to a new, redeemed life requires a holy, grateful, willing submission, agreed upon from a met yearning for God. Do any of us pull that off? Meeting God in this life leads to this awesome and shocking agreement to forgo this life to be with him. This is not a suicidal pact but a cooperative venture to live as God leads us. I don't know the stats on that. How could I? I can say, though, when we're at our best we can offer eager acceptance to our creator if we know upon our death that we go to meet him.

Most of us are merely grateful but rarely willing. We grudgingly accept death, as a last resort, submitting to its inevitability while firmly angry at its purpose. Death is uncalled for. Our gratefulness is likely not the mature kind, where our death can be used in any way that God sees fit. Because few of us pass on with a cheerful demeaner, we force ourselves to be amiable for those who watch us die. That's not heroic. An amicable death is just good manners.

The animal world, our non-human travelers on earth's journey, are no better witnesses in this last of tasks. They grovel, moan, wail, and shriek like humans do. Because of that similarity in leaving this life many of us wonder if animals enjoy the same hope we have for eternal life? Shouldn't they?

Hope for eternal life, I believe, is losing popularity. More and more doubt the truth of such a thing. Meanwhile, animals don't seem to know anything about eternity. Their hopes live entirely in the moment, though building nests, migrating thousands of miles, and birthing families looks a lot like hope to me.

Rather than go with gracious compliance, we humans are likely only grateful for an end to suffering, worry, and violence. So too, the animals. I suspect, or more appropriately expect, that the minimum of gratitude is probably enough for God, if mercy is real. Due to the sheer numbers of lives lost under interminable circumstances, the exercise for mercy, allowing us a better life, seems necessary.

The other half of a holy exit—our willing submission to death's last gasp—only takes place if the options for the next life are clear and there's time to ponder it. Maybe not clear but hoped for. How many of us have that hope? I suppose hope is present more than certainty. What calculator can we use to figure out the proper time to die willingly? Again, mercy must be God's primary tool for redemption.

Animals confirm the atrocities of death. They also seldom have the opportunity for a holy submission, bound up in hope. They do yearn, though, to no longer be eaten, to no longer kill in order to survive. Any study of animals finds that they enjoy each other when their stomachs are full. Violence comes from being wary and predatory, not from being satisfied. Happy creatures run in circles like newborns when they get simple things, like a drink of water. When given the choice, semi-to-fully sentient creatures would grasp the opportunity to choose life in paradise among all living creatures with glee. Does that, in fact, happen for animals? I'm prone to think it does.

More importantly, do all non-human creatures agree, and accept that offer? That's a frightening, terrible thing to consider, envisioning that some would choose their old life of killing, eating, and existing in a violent way over heaven with God. We know such a decision may be true for belligerent humans. Belligerent because they know better but reportedly do not want eternal life.

Those of intractable belligerence would not include humans and animals that have been poisoned in their attitudes and beliefs. These damaged creatures have been improperly formed. God must have other plans of a merciful sort for them. Worse than all others are those abused into deep,

deep dismay over the hope for a good and merciful God. The tortured are primed for mercy.

Those who reject God want to be left alone by everyone. People who don't know about God don't count as bereft of mercy. One cannot reject what one doesn't know. One theory is that all are eventually won over by God when he shows himself to them in the next life. God has every antidote for the worst of poisons. That might be the truth for everyone and everything.

Still, there might be truly evil humans whom God can never reach. People who have attached themselves to evil without remorse. Maybe it's also true for animals. Might be. Maybe there aren't any people or animals like that. God could possibly be so good at love that he eventually gets his strings into all of us. Eventually. Does everyone eventually repent?

Snarl doesn't answer that question. The book presupposes that God takes care of the extent and reach of mercy. For literary purposes, and because I have almost convinced myself of the preposterous notion that animals will see redemption, *Snarl* presumes what we get is what animals also get. In telling what animals will experience in this life and the next, then, *Snarl* imagines what we can see for ourselves, what true and wonderful things might happen for us.

The good. The bad. The option and the possibility of a wholesome, wonderful eternity. Or, I've just taken poetic license into a realm where the licensing does not count. We get either a wholesome eternity for animals and us, or some other thing that falls short of my understanding about God.

We'll find out.

Acknowledgements

In 2014, my lovely and youngest daughter Jenelle and my beloved Joanne read the first draft of *Snarl* with furrowed brows and worried eyes. I watched them while breathing slowly, sneaking peaks at their reactions. Their faces said everything. I hid behind objects, trying to disappear.

Joanne touched me on the shoulder, dismissing the amateurish draft, and said she wanted to read the rest of it.

Forty years I've been doing this. Analyzing the signs of my test readers, my dear friends and family who cannot escape from me. Meanwhile, no bites from publishers. Journalism, ghost writing, magazines, technical documentation, and marketing copy honed parts of the writing craft that paid me. I got plenty of that work.

Snarl sits in the middle of a string of novels. I've begun two more novels since I wrote the completed draft of *Snarl* in 2015. From then until 2021 my harkens shouted only at deaf ears. Crickets from the publishing world.

Dan Rector, a friend from Colorado, spiked my reading list in 2016 with *On Writing* by Stephen King. "If you still want to be a writer after reading that, then you should continue writing. Otherwise, hang it up," he said. Dan then read the second, more full draft of *Snarl*. With care and concern he told me three or four things I needed to do with the book. I remember only "hook" from all that he said. I didn't have a hook.

"I thought you didn't like Stephen King," Joanne asked me.

"It doesn't matter. His book *On Writing* is gold," I said.

A few years later, Steve Hall, a wonderful friend and blog pal of mine at www.homelesscatholic.com, read the next draft. His reaction deserved a hug, but I held back. We don't hug.

"When's the sequel to this book?" he said. Serious.

He skipped over all the terrible errors and lousy flow.

"It's in my head," he said.

ACKNOWLEDGEMENTS

My four decades of writing came in bursts, each followed by chagrin, doubt, and nonsensical rationalizations. In 2017, I said, "I can write for free now. I'm retired."

Two years ago, Ronda Chervin read *Snarl*. She asked to read something I was working on. Ronda was my philosophy professor at Loyola Marymount University in the early 1970's. She's a wonderful evangelist for the Catholic Church and written four dozen books on the subject. Joanne and I kept in touch with her for fifty years. She read a further post-Steve semi-polished version of *Snarl*. She gushed over the thing, so kind, so lovely to express her unique Ronda-like enjoyment for the story.

"Ronda is right," Joanne said. "See? What did I tell you?"

Jerry Derloshon, my oldest friend, dating back to St. John Bosco High School in California, read the version I sent to Ronda. Jerry is a great enabler, a witty million-dollar-smile guy. He's been published. He's relentless and he encouraged me to hang in there. As a hoot, he wrote the first promo paragraph for Snarl. I use it because I love Jerry, and he's really good at copywriting. "Keep sending the manuscript out there." he said. He's not pushy. He's just a really great guy. If you don't have a Jerry, get one.

I set aside expected pain of vain hope when I asked Xander Redfern in 2015 if he would create illustrations for the book. He's the best tattoo artist on the planet. He's my son-in-law and loves my oldest daughter. I will do anything for him, but I have no tattoos. Instead, I tell people I'm pretty sure he's the best. "It's the canvas that pays," Xander says. I understand, more than he knows. He agreed to draw for me and drafted three of a possible seven drawings. I loved them, and told him when it gets a publishing date I'll give him the heads up.

Seven years later, March of 2022, Wipf & Stock sent me a contract. I gave Xander the good news.

Debbie Warhola, a journalist who worked for us 40 years ago, agreed to copyedit the book. She is an accomplished journalist at The Gazette in Colorado Springs. Debbie was so helpful. I had slogged through Grammarly scans, made plot adjustments, and plowed through cause and effect details. She got her hands on the manuscript and a week later handed me a huge new pile of work to do. I am Debbie's biggest fan.

I approached Tim Fuller for a read, a friend found from a book club organized by Martin Nussbaum, just a few weeks ago. He said he would read it and write something "appropriate." It's the best Forward a book with an unconfirmed premise could hope for. I get goosebumps every time I read it.

Back in March, when Joanne smiled after I told her about Matt Wimer's email offering a contract for *Snarl*, her happiness grew my heart. She isn't a hop up and down jumper, or a fist bumper. She just smiles at you so hard that you know what heaven is like. God took a picture of that smile and put it on his fridge for relieved wives.

I imagine for my own reasons that my dead relatives and friends have seen the picture and nodded their approval. Add in old pets, ridden horses, and formerly eaten fowls restored to happy existences around them to complete the scene.

My children are happy about the book. My siblings, too. Good friends have been so supportive. You'll hopefully see their names writing gushing recommendations on the web. What burden my hubris places upon them. Marketing at Wipf & Stock will be pleased, though.

Through it all, Joanne's gotten as much enjoyment about the publication opportunity as I have.

"What a good woman she is," people tell me.

I know.

John Pearring
April, 2022

On the heels of Pleistocene extinctions ten thousand years ago the North American mountain lion emerged from a swath of ancestors. Puma, leopard, lynx, and jaguar bred from among the trees and rocks a fierce ruler, the inimitable cougar. Cagey from evolution, compact in form, the mountain lion took charge of the land's harvest, corralling large and small animals.

Keenly aware of the domestic plans wrought by oncoming, over-breeding humans, the mountain lion retreated into the havens of hill and boulder. This serious package of beast and jurisdiction creeps back and forward to the edges of man's dangerous environs as humans migrate into the assigned domains of the cougar.

Thus, the species of man and lion grew up together, migrating from the Northern Yukon through both Rockies and Appalachia to the lower continent's Andes. Over thousands of years, they matched personalities as the masters of every moving thing. Each feared the other. They listened to God's careful whispers as their ancestors prompted them. Or, man and beast harkened instead to evil's violent and insidious urges as coarser natures consumed their behavior.

Humans and cougar lived this divine versus demonic challenge under the murky influence and shifting foundation of family, friends, foes, and fiends. Few arthropods and animals saw good and evil so clearly. Those who did were courageous, devoted, and somehow aware of a coming treasure that awaits everyone, even amidst sure and constant chaos.

Chapter One

SEPARATION

Shall I reckon up for you the differences of the other animals, both from us and from each other — differences of nature, and of production, and of region, and of temper, and as it were of social life? How is it that some are gregarious and others solitary, some herbivorous and others carnivorous, some fierce and others tame, some fond of man and domesticated, others untamable and free? And some we might call bordering on reason and power of learning, while others are altogether destitute of reason . . . some strong, others weak, some apt at self-defense, others timid and crafty . . . some attached to one spot, some amphibious; some delight in beauty and others are unadorned . . . Is this not the clearest proof of the majestic working of God?

—St. Gregory Nazianzen, Second Theological Oration (Oration 28), #'s 23-26, a.d. 381

STARE

Stare pondered, stretched out on a resting spot. Legs opened behind her, she lay in an awkward way, spread in resignation more than rest. She'd been there all day, doing nothing requiring effort, remembering, sleeping, and unsure of way too many things. Not typical lion behavior.

Her cubs returned at day's end, pattered about in silence for a few moments, quick glimpses her way as they circled. They finally settled in front of her. The three mountain lions formed a triangle, heads facing, paws crossed under their chins.

When on all fours, the cubs stood as tall as Stare, except their youthful skin rippled with muscles. Stare was old for a lion in the wild, a mark of successful survival and less time left. Her depleted body sagged under the weight of hanging fir. She no longer swayed as she walked, which seldom happened anymore.

A fly landed on her snout. Too tired to open her mouth and flick at it with her tongue, Stare watched instead. Her eyes crossed as she tried to focus.

She saw beyond the bold fly and noticed her oldest cub, Snarl, looking her way, head still on his forepaws. His long, stiff eyebrows twitched. The senior male in their small family, Snarl could claim inherited advantages not found in any other pack member. Stare wasn't sure if Snarl realized it yet. He was the dominant species in the dry, dusty green mountains below and a handful of miles north of what the humans called Pikes Peak. Snarl didn't know that. Neither the name of the mountain nor his dominance among living things.

Stare also had no idea what humans called the mountain that rose above and to the south of where they lived. Names don't work that way for lions. Human thought, intentions, and motives never crossed her mind. She had always been outstanding, though, at how lions thought about things. Until now. Her mind wandered, shifting from moment to moment, sliding away from present matters. Once certain of almost every detail about her life, her cubs, and their surroundings, Stare now questioned minor decisions, aware less and less of the big ones.

The ridged crevasse where they lay had been her summer home for a dozen years. Winter caves and hidden holes dotted the high ground of her canyon. As for the humans, she hadn't seen one for some time. Purposely and cleverly, she found this rugged terrain which so far humans had avoided. Her last several broods birthed unseen in this rough, steeply granite-lined chasm with juts of flat spaces to lounge about and scan their tiny empire. All else — encroaching developments, roadways, and cabins — remained distant.

Deer, varmints, the occasional elk, and rabbits filled their bellies.

Snarl would eventually meet humans, Stare assumed. She did not train either cub regarding the ways of humans because had no idea how to do that, other than hide. The two boys would have to figure them out on their own.

Her elder cub found privilege simply by his luck of birth. Snarl moved when and where he wanted, with little concern for interference. Stare wondered where he would go. He would have to go, of course. None of her cubs had stayed, even when they wanted to. She hadn't let them.

Stare blended into the earth, outright gray with only small tinged patches of the cougar's orange fur. As a young mother, she sported a thin rake of gray on a bronzed body. Stare's elders and her cubs carried the same family trait, quadruple strips of light fur between the front shoulders. The pack's mark was no longer visible on Stare, even in watery reflections. All of her had gone gray.

What brought that up, she asked herself? Her mind shifted from one thing to another. She had forgotten what happens next with the cubs. She resigned some time ago to let the oldest do what he wanted. Thankfully, she had taught him most of what she knew before her body began this current decline. She relinquished control without knowing if Snarl was ready because she had no other choice.

How many kittens had she birthed in her turns at the seasons? She could not remember. Were there always just male cubs? No females came to mind. Her memories had faded along with her instincts. The worry of the night, a typical thought at day's end, had also lessened. Stare doubted herself, wavered in certainty. Even her steady, consistent drive to care for the cubs evaded Stare's grasp. She spent her time scratching in the dirt and sleeping.

A worry nagged at her thoughts. The cubs had grown overly large. Less cub, more lion. Maybe she was shrinking. The oldest reached her height and length. Though he came only one full moon later, the youngest, Spit — too late to be called a twin — almost matched his brother's size.

The boys did not resemble each other in any way. The younger constantly moved, boisterous and spontaneous to a fault. Spit baffled Stare. He was willing to obey like Snarl, yet unable to focus on anything without great effort. Spit's body squeezed tight from snout to back paws, poised to pounce. He scrunched his lids shut rather than let them fall. Spit knew when to nap, but struggled to even do that.

Stare's older cub was pensive and reflective, though a lion has no words or concept for such behavior. Snarl looked squarely at his mother in recent months, like he was doing now. Stare compared this look to Snarl's odd, gnarled pup face. The memory, still there, reminded Stare about Snarl's natural ability to dominate. As a pup, Snarl searched her eyes for direction or approval. Now, his gaze exhibited confidence, a mix of learning and instinct, the demeanor of a self-aware male. She knew nothing of either learning or instinct as separate kinds of behaviors, other than the result.

Stare shivered. She conjured violent memories of dominant male lions. They were dangerous. She had waited too long, Stare thought. Snarl should be on his own.

She thought about his patterns. Snarl marked his territory without Stare's urging and assumed control of situations simply with the lock of his head. This was the way with more muscular males when they gazed at both fellow lions and prey. She didn't teach him this. It came from some primal formation, like the sturdiness of mature trees compared to young saplings.

Snarl looked at Stare longer than she wanted. She turned her head away. The worn mother realized, frightened at her forgetfulness, that this change in Snarl had been going on for a while. She no longer attempted to stare along with him, assuring him, because his assurance had already been confirmed.

With her face down, she returned to pondering.

She named him Snarl, an image of his face rather than a name. That's how lions recognize each other, a likeness that sticks. Stare wasn't sure if "Snarl" fit him now. He rarely needed to be aggressive. His presence was enough. Animal recognition and identification begins with a visage that will morph over time. An original visual picture, added with smells, sounds, and body movements, fix a memory that stays in place. Stare wouldn't change the visage of her son. Snarl would always be Snarl.

As a very young lion, the fur on Snarl's face curled as if he had too much skin. The grimace eventually melted away. His face now held one un-moving, non-emotional profile. With a sullen fixed gaze, Snarl established control over everything he could see. Growls seldom came from his lanky, self-controlled frame. He lightly lifted a paw to move something aside, or to stay Spit. Snarl's movements were easy, flowing, and focused.

Spit . . . well, Spit was not that way.

Her two cubs were the least difficult to mother in her memory. It's Snarl's exceptional mood control, she reckoned. He didn't flinch at Spit's uncalled-for jumps or swipes. Short tempers burden mother lions and age them quickly as they must match violence with violence. She either did little to raise them or taught them on a fully formed motherly cruise control. Spit no longer required her discipline. Snarl paused Spit's outbursts with a head movement, effortlessly eliminating further unwelcome behavior.

Snarl and Spit would be her last since no male would find any scent on her worth chasing. Her elderly body showed few signs of life. She scratched at the dirt again because her body tinged in pain that neither licking nor stretching relieved.

The cubs hunted on their own, and she remained here sleeping. Stare didn't forage food because she went nowhere. They long ago stopped whining at her. Hunting did not interest her. She tried to recall the last hunt where she had led them.

She looked again at Spit and saw meat left in the dust, not far from her. She frowned at the food. Spit, or maybe it was Snarl, seemed to repeatedly leave uneaten, unfinished food whenever they came back.

She wondered how long they had been in this place. They should change their resting spot. She tried to remember where she planned their winter den this year.

She watched Spit pounce on the meat, unleashed by a force she couldn't see. A leg of a deer. Spit dragged it away. Stare thought Spit must know she disliked meat in the open.

Stare recalled Spit's noises. The pup ate anytime, even early in the mornings, like a wolf staying near a kill. Lions should return to a hidden kill many times like she had shown them. Spit could eat, but had he actually made the kill?

Stare did not understand Spit. His patterns amused her when he was younger, but this must not continue. On his own, the coyotes, wolves, and bears would overcome him. He was most vulnerable when eating.

Had they shifted resting places, she wondered? The cubs had gotten older, she remembered again. Stare was alarmed because she had an uncontrollable urge to stay put. She couldn't muster the energy to move. The boys did not look like cubs anymore. No more spots or visible rings on their tails.

She lifted her head. Snarl did the same. She must either leave them or hope they leave her. The cubs no longer played together, certainly not over this past winter, and the last time one cuddled his head upon her neck, the weight had strained too much. She growled him away. Strangely, she remembered, that cub had been Snarl.

What must she do now? Stare's body had always given her the signs of what was next, like the scent that would attract a male, or the sour sweat from harboring kittens inside her. What was her body saying now?

She lowered her head back onto her forelegs. She sighed into the dirt, and a dust cloud puffed forward.

Snarl peered at her through the mist of dirt. She watched him as he put his head back down on his forelegs, just like her, still staring. He mimicked her sigh, she thought, as dust flew away from the snuff of his nostrils.

Out of courtesy to his increasingly dominant role and her many years of learned fear, she turned away again.

Snarl watched his mother, convinced that she no longer thought about him or wondered what he was doing. The sadness overwhelmed him.

He wanted to see into her and her to see into him. Snarl had fallen asleep most of his life with the eyes of his mother upon him. He would drift off, glancing at her, knowing she was there when he couldn't keep his eyelids open any longer.

As a cub, he would stride through tall grass and watch for her nod or correction. Am I quiet enough? Are my shoulders below the seedy tips, swaying in the same pattern where I do not walk?

Snarl's first kill, an effortless drop of his paw upon a rabbit as big as his torso, drew a look from her that he would remember for the rest of his life. She cocked her head in amazement. He recalled it once again with pride.

He climbed a tree as a very young cub, and he checked for her approval at every branch. When he fell, she nudged him back up, and he more carefully took the tree with leaps rather than grasping wildly. Her head reached high as he stood on the most extended branch, masking his fear by watching her closely.

Not recently, though. Stare turned away from him, and nothing he did kept her attention. Something had changed in her, he thought. She ate little, and now nothing.

He brought her leftover food, setting it not too close. He had a deep respect for her keen abilities to provide for him and Spit and did not want to insult her. When she would not eat, he purred lightly to Spit, allowing him to finish it. His mother would not let uneaten food in their den or their resting spots. Left out food happened regularly, now. Not acceptable for either his mother or for Spit.

Spit had a bottomless stomach. He required twice what Snarl considered an average meal. So many wasted movements and high energy. Spit would be a very busy hunter.

When his mother puffed the dirt in front of her head, seemingly burdened by the weight of it, Snarl found himself dropping his head too. He figured she did not want him around anymore and apparently would be better off quiet and alone. Maybe she needed to recover from their constant presence, even though they did not expect anything from her anymore.

On the other hand, perhaps she would regain her appetite and her hearing. Snarl had no reason to think otherwise, until now. He sensed that not only was his mother changing, but everything might be different. He set aside the thought.

Snarl grunted to Spit, a noise that Spit would know. The two had exchanged this semi-growl communication since his first memories. They used an unexplained gruff language that made sense to the two of them. At one time, the grunting purr called out where they were — to watch out for each other. The purpose changed. Now, they knew that the shared noise defined not just where they were but where the other must not go.

Eventually, Snarl and Spit would keep each other at bay with this noise, Snarl realized. He understood the difference from their younger playfulness, though the importance of staying clear from each other confused him. Except for the food. The amount of food that Spit needed outpaced Snarl's intake. They had gotten bigger. The brothers could not cover the same range and have enough to eat.

Snarl watched his brother drag off to a space behind where he sat to devour the deer leg remains. They chased off several coyotes who had downed a mid-aged buck. It had no broken leg, no deformity. He knew why coyotes sometimes attacked healthy deer. Reckless kills came from hunger. Snarl looked at his mother and purred to her. She lifted her head, and so did he. He wanted her to see that he remembered things like that.

She did not purr back. She looked at Spit instead.

His mother no longer heard their communication. Her hearing must be going with her appetite, Snarl thought. This attempt to feed her must stop. Too dangerous. Snarl would no longer bring food for his mother or Spit. She did not want the food. He had to respect that. Spit needed to find food on his own.

She laid her head back on her paws. Snarl did the same. He snuffed a sigh, and a cloud of dust like his mother's puffed outward and then slowly floated into the air.

Spit's muscles twitched, and his head kept bobbing. It was time to lie still. How could his mother and his brother do it? He forced himself to stay where he was, though everything in his body wanted to run and dart in the twilight.

The smell of the meat added to the nervous itching of his fur. What was this test? Mother didn't want it. Spit wanted it.

He stared at the food, waiting to hear from Snarl. Always this waiting game with him.

"Prrr . . . grrr . . . prrrrr." Snarl signaled to Spit.

Spit leaped high and far, enjoying a welcome relief from the awful still-ness, extending his body as he flew at the meat. Finally. More food to eat in the evening.

He was famished.

NO MOON

White dots sparkled in the night sky, but that's not where the Great Horned owl was looking. He studied the forest floor. The smaller animals knew him by his noise. They called him Grunt. Mice, babies of any species, and even skunks would only move about when they heard his call. His hoot was a guttural, staccato triple set of low-sounding growls. Each species mimicked Grunt's signature hoot, compelled to warn others. They traveled during his hoots, and froze in the silence. From experience, they believed he couldn't hoot and track them at the same time.

Grunt continued watching below, eyeing the ground since the sun had set. The darkness limited his catch of rodents. There would be no birds now. He displayed little emotion, but his occasional hooting expressed periodic reminders to other owls that this is not where they should be perched. When he hooted, Grunt scouted for rustling in the trees in case he spied a challenge to his territory.

Tonight was a good time for a brawl with a more significant catch, he considered. There was no moon. He was hungry. The forest was dry, limiting meals for several days to just bugs. Grunt scanned the forest floor beneath his perch in the tallest Blue Spruce from his favorite standing on a Colorado mountain ridge. Every moving thing stayed still, hiding on the ground.

Grunt's ears and eyebrows angled off the top of his head, warning any-one who looked his way. Though he had probably never seen his reflection, he sported a scowl with practiced intensity, an obnoxious superiority. Or so say the falcons.

He heard the padding of large paws making their way through the trees below him. That rhythm of two-by-two paw placement, firmly press-ing down the spruce needles in the rocky soil, could mean only one animal — a mountain lion.

Uncontrollably, Grunt reacted, flapped his wings and gripped the sturdy bark on his spot, safely above the lion. The owl couldn't smell and didn't know that he couldn't. However, the plodding of the creature below him was irregular, unsure. He figured the lion was either ill or confused. His wings flapped again, more wildly this time. The lion had distracted the owl. The forest floor animals scuttered about, less afraid of the preoccupied owl than the more dangerous lion.

A female skunk in the bushes below the owl knew to remain still — her best defense from both the lion and Grunt. She could smell the pallor of death on the lion who ambled awkwardly just a few feet from her. What a sight. The mother skunk's front feet stretched out before. She held them stiffly after covering them in leaves. She watched the lion's labored movements. It walked by her, across a path deer had made, stumbling for several yards, then stepped effortlessly over the ridge's edge.

The skunk caught a glimpse of the owl's wingspan swooping off the tree above her. She knew the coast was clear and could now head toward home to the converted wood-rat hole where her three babies waited for her. The owl was gone, leaving an opening to catch a rodent meal on the way. She saw them running everywhere.

GONE

Spit stood rocking on his forelegs, surveying where his mother had lain when he last saw her. Agitated, his glassy eyes darted about and then back to the ground where he could imagine her outline. He repeated this over and over, perplexed. His head swayed in confusion.

Spit saw her outline pressed into the soft red clay, and where her claws had scratched in the dirt. Her head had rested across the marks of her forelegs. Spit could even see where her whiskers had twitched a dusty furrow. Fur lay in a few places, gray speckled tufts.

He looked left and right into the woods, away from the cover of the great pine boughs above him. His mother has been gone all morning. Spit sniffed the formed pattern of grass and red dirt where she had recently spent most of her time, trying to figure out how long ago she had been there. He couldn't tell because he had never learned such things.

Spit sensed something had gone wrong but couldn't figure out what. Stare was usually here, sleeping through most of the day, and now she wasn't. It made no sense to him.

Snarl walked toward Spit, unnoticed until Snarl bumped him in the side. Spit darted out of Snarl's way, cowering.

Snarl looked at Spit with his familiar slow, intent gaze, but nothing else showed in his eyes. Spit hesitantly stepped over to his mother's usual spot, looked at Snarl, and stepped back. Can't you see, Spit asked in his motions? Snarl reflected nothing. Spit began rocking again. He wanted an explanation, an update on his mother. Though difficult for him, he stopped rocking, shaking just a bit, and stretched his head toward his brother, searching for an answer in Snarl's eyes.

Snarl's shoulders lifted from their standard, head down slouch. Spit watched his brother look beyond the trees and brush from their hillside spot. Spit followed his eyes. Snarl's head stopped every few seconds as he peered into the distance. Spit waited expectantly. He wondered if Snarl knew where she was.

Snarl periodically looked back at Spit, which bothered Spit immensely. His brother's face had become deeply intimidating. Then Snarl would shift back to gaze at something in the distance, squinting as he searched into the trees. Snarl's eyes softened and hardened, back and forth, reviewing something in his mind. Spit's brother was always in his mind. Slow to act when there was time. Snarl waited too long for the impatient Spit. Always too long.

Spit's body shook, nervous twitches everywhere. Spit wanted his brother to act quickly. They were wasting time. What had happened to her? Where was she? They needed to find her. She had always been with them. He grunted a few times at his brother, worried that they were just standing around. He shivered uncontrollably. Spit didn't know what was wrong with his body. He wanted his mother.

Snarl faced his shaky brother. He didn't return a grunt, not even a low rumble. Spit's older brother had become less verbal. He had adopted facial expressions that all looked the same. Spit didn't recognize this new look, though. Snarl's eyes were focusing, searing into him.

Oh. That look reminded Spit of their mother. Maybe he just imagined it.

Snarl dropped his head just a bit but the movement down and toward Spit, his mouth closed, was frightening. From his shoulders down to his paws, Spit shook. He was confused and worried, both from the loss of his mother and Snarl's stare.

Spit whined, pitifully, like a pup. He couldn't control it. The whine seemed to come out of every part of him. It was Snarl's eyes. They were so much like mother.

When he first noticed Spit standing over his mother's resting place, rocking left and right, like a lizard, Snarl concluded that Stare had left them. Snarl had paced around the area while Spit slept. He'd walked in circles for hours. He had no idea where their mother had gone.

He knew that Spit must not stay here, though, and neither should he.

Spit acted like an abandoned cub. Snarl decided that he needed to get away from their over-stayed spot. His mother would have considered that. She, though, was not there. Dangers piled up when they stayed in one place. He wondered if he could think like her, like the mother of cubs. She had not been careful lately.

No, Snarl wasn't like her. He could imagine her response but could not respond like her. Snarl was not comfortable.

He could not help Spit understand that their mother was gone if they stayed. They no longer had a caretaker. Snarl knew he was not a caretaker. He knew nothing about that. That was what the mother did. Spit was confused, helpless, and had begun to cry. Taking care of Spit was not a job he could do. Snarl was sure of that.

He looked into the horizon away from the sun. They needed to live without a caretaker, beginning right now. From what Snarl knew, male adult lions did not live together. They had to manage their territories alone. Snarl knew that but was reasonably sure that Spit did not.

He looked at his brother and then out where they must go. They must travel opposite from the trail of the sun. Under the sun's path, the weather changed. It got warmer down there, where more lions would migrate. Snarl looked at Spit's rocking body. Still too much pup in him. They must go away from other lions.

He also knew that the two of them needed to separate. A good thing for Snarl. A requirement. Not so much for Spit.

Snarl considered the options. Spit might be able to live and hunt this familiar ground. Only this current territory would be well-known to him. That meant Snarl needed to be elsewhere. He gazed toward the mountain ridges into the blue part of the sky. That was where he must go.

He turned his head to Spit again. Snarl considered that his brother might not survive, a likely outcome, considering his poorly learned skills. Snarl did not like that possibility. He had always watched out for Spit. Their mother approved when he did. His brother was somewhat annoying, but that was not the reason to leave him. Snarl did not know about being a mother.

Suddenly, something deep inside Snarl, a decision that he knew was not his own, appeared to him. He might need to kill his brother. The idea startled him. It was a charged feeling, a rushing emotion, from a dark influence he had experienced before. Snarl did not trust dark compulsions.

When he was a very young cub, Snarl's mother turned away from him when he would react carelessly to random urges. The young lion snarled at everything, swiping at the air, and attacked with a fierceness that froze animals in their tracks. He could tell she disapproved, though. He wanted to please her.

Spit seemed to have no other kind of activity. He flailed wildly at everything, from gnats to kicking deer. Spit's behavior, different from Snarl, seemed unprovoked, more ridiculous than dangerous. His mother paid no attention to Spit's personality. Snarl was confused about that. Their mother disapproved, but Spit didn't behave any differently.

Snarl studied his confusing brother. His fur quaked like a trapped rabbit. Snarl stared into the frightened eyes of Spit to calm both his own dark urges and his brother's distress. Snarl also missed his mother. He lowered his head to get his brother's attention and waited for another more acceptable idea. Killing his brother seemed compelling but resistible.

Snarl measured his actions with practiced detachment.

Another, better sense finally rose within Snarl when he held back the rushing urges. Patience. Better purposes grew more significant than the compelling dark desires. He didn't think killing his brother was a good idea. So, he waited.

The patient sense moved slowly, though, and took time to deliver information to him. He needed a more helpful prompting. Sometimes, just one other thing would develop when he waited out a dark urge. Other times, several options would pop up. This time, one developed. He would do that, then, instead of the dark compulsion.

While both senses battled within him, Snarl peered deeper into Spit's eyes.

The rushing urges twitched the muscles in his shoulders but did not get to his limbs. He had not allowed that to happen for quite some time. Impatience expected him to leap, to swing his paws, and to rumble his voice. Patience sparked all his senses, but not his muscles. He did not need to worry about stiffening his muscles when needed. His muscles were always ready.

Snarl could smell the dry, dank sage strong in even the faintest wind. He heard leaves lightly rustling, close to the blank silence of morning turning to a full day's sun. His brother cowered, but Snarl knew he had resisted the strange desire to kill him simply by letting time pass. Spit wailed.

Snarl knew what to do next.

He lifted his head, snuffing at the air. The patient reaction was always better. The practice to wait had made him more aware, and Snarl trusted everything about that.

THE BROTHERS MOVE

Spit watched Snarl as his brother lowered his nostrils to the ground and began walking toward what humans called north and west, down a small ridge and up to another. Lions identified direction by the sun, the colors of the sky, and the wind. Spit followed. Snarl's steps seemed almost plodding to Spit's pattered hopping. Still, he stayed behind his older brother, attempting to keep the slow, steady pace so unfamiliar to Spit's standard travel patterns.

Their traverse through the mountains, a quiet straight plod, unnerved Spit, who preferred to shift from left to right, periodically crawling and jumping rather than moving in a direct line. He felt compromised traveling this way but decided that the two of them were more than safe against danger. Still, to calm his nerves, he moved slightly left and right of Snarl to look ahead and around him.

They walked several miles, farther north from the Sun behind them, and then entered unfamiliar territory. Snarl kept walking. Spit followed, longer than he had imagined walking. He looked back, still aware of where they had been but less so with each new step. He relied upon Snarl to navigate but Snarl's pace worried Spit.

The sun moved across the sky, shining over Spit's right shoulder across to his left flank. Spit looked back as they traveled forward, thinking he should stop. He did not know where else to go, though. His breath came in shorter gulps, and his tongue hung farther out, lying across the left teeth of his snout.

Snarl finally slowed down at the edge of a cliff. The path, likely made by deer, ended there. Snarl stopped and turned to his brother. Spit thought maybe Snarl was angry at him. He couldn't tell. Usually, Spit would turn his head away from Snarl's stare. Instead, tuckered out, Spit kept eye contact as Snarl walked to him.

Snarl stepped inches from Spit and slowly pressed his forehead onto Spit's face. They were almost the same size now. Spit was shaking. He wanted to run, but the warmth of his brother's head on his and Snarl's slow breathing calmed him down. Spit closed his eyes upon his brother's snout. They stood that way for several minutes until Spit looked up, blinking at his brother, their eyes so close together.

Snarl didn't blink. He never really seemed to anymore. They stared into each other's eyes. Snarl then growled, low, and pressed his forehead onto Spit's face. Spit began to shake again but he was afraid to turn away. He did not know what Snarl was doing.

Snarl licked him on both sides of his face as they used to when they were little, all while their foreheads were pressed together. The pressure from Snarl's forehead forced Spit to step backward, and Snarl kept pushing, pressing foreheads and licking and growling low.

Spit continued to step backward, confused. He felt the warm breath of his brother, his head upon his, pushing him back. Exhausted from the long walk and weak from the tension caused by Snarl's pressure on his head, Spit fell back on his haunches. Groggy, he wavered and fell over.

After only a few seconds, Spit mustered enough strength to get back up on his front legs, and sat on his butt. His stomach growled. He was dizzy and weak from hunger.

Snarl emitted several low growls and bobbed his head. The movements mesmerized the younger lion, and Spit watched in a daze as his brother finally backed up and turned away. Snarl looked back at Spit only once and then effortlessly bounded over the cliff at the end of the path and disappeared from Spit's sight.

After deciding what to do about his brother, Snarl turned his attention to what lay ahead of him.

Snarl left the only hunting spot he had ever known, sure of his decision, convinced that his mother was not coming back. He'd decided to head away from the path of the sun to mark out new territory for himself. His brother would need to fend for himself because the dark urges, though shocking, properly prodded him to separate from his brother.

The dark feelings in his head began to recede as soon as he left the camp.

He reminisced about the few trips where his mother had taken them upland. That direction made sense. Snarl had been to the upper edge of his mother's territory for a reason, he concluded. This very reason. Spit would likely honor this break between them, not because he fully understood, rather because the dangerous canyon area ahead would keep Spit from going further.

Snarl began his steady trod away from the sun, toward where the horizon showed the darkest. A ridge of two canyons lined the upland parameter where he had learned to hunt. Antelope wandered into the eastern and smaller canyon. Snarl had been taught not to head down there. Too risky. Coyotes and wolves hid in dens there.

Snarl could survive better farther away than Spit. So, that was it. Spit would own the familiar territory, and Snarl would take the more challenging. It was right. This would be the way his mother would want it.

Today Snarl would allow the old territory as hunting grounds for his brother. If the younger lion could survive, he would need this gift. The area beyond this canyon, and maybe several canyons ahead, would become Snarl's domain. He might have to win it from another animal and cross dangerous divides to find the right place. Even though this was all he could do for his brother, it was surely enough.

He began his trek, head steady and body following.

Snarl heard Spit tagging along behind but disregarded him, expecting him to bound off east or west, or more likely just go back. Spit's mother would not purr to him today, would not set a path for the rambunctious cat. Not this time. Snarl plodded along in his ready cadence, sparing energy, and tuned in to his surroundings. He studied what he could see, smell, or feel on his tender whiskers, swinging tail, and padded feet. He expected Spit to whine and turn back at any time. The sun moved across the sky behind him as he kept moving. Spit, though, stayed with him moving a little bit left and right, yet on the path, remaining close.

Surprising, thought Snarl.

They walked for several hours. The forest quieted before them, two lions ambling in parade. Snarl glanced at memory after memory, fewer as they continued. The warm rock outcropping, tiny nourishing springs, and many small creature-havens were all familiar. His mother taught them to harvest when the population of their prey seemed to step upon themselves.

Snarl did not stop. Several times he felt Spit move toward a spring or an animal hovel. Still, he'd come back, panting harder each time, his energy ebbing away, too quickly. How did he not realize the toll on his reserves?

The memories thinned for Snarl as they followed deer trails further into the wooded hillsides. He didn't stop to study the scat and disturbances of leaves, tripped branches, and bruised Kinnikinnik. Usually storing this information about the plants and trampled land, Snarl instead set aside a visual recording. Rather, he thought about the new images and territory he would soon learn, with both feelings of worry and wonder churning with each step he took.

Spit's breathing now had a rasp to it. Dry. Snarl spied the end of his known territory, the farthest he had followed his mother. At the edge of their territory, the long canyon lay before him, sliced left up in an increasing fracture, dropping wider at his right, into the flatter prairies below. Only his mother had ever gone down there. He had stood at this very spot, waiting for her.

The still air in the canyon hung peppered with dust. This was a most uninviting place.

Snarl slowed as he rimmed the ridge of the canyon. He felt Spit's labored breath just inches behind him. The younger lion had almost bumped into him when Snarl stopped. He turned around. The face of his younger sibling hung gaunt, with reddened eyes. Spit stood uncertain, still confused. He needed to eat. Snarl watched him, wondering what his brother would do without him. Spit did not look away from Snarl, surprising the older brother. Spit seemed to be expecting Snarl to do something.

Ah, to take charge. Spit was thinking like someone still under a caretaker.

No. Brother lions could not be like this. Snarl could not be a mother lion to his brother. This wouldn't do. Snarl slowly moved toward his brother, eyes locked, closing in eyeballs to eyeballs, snouts down until their foreheads touched. He pushed his brother backward, repeating the steps, slowly moving Spit back.

Snarl sensed that Spit was confused, and he licked his brother's face, moistened his dry, red eyes with his long tongue. He pushed Spit to go back on the trail, signaling that this was as far as Spit should go.

Repeatedly and gently, Snarl connected foreheads and urged his brother backward, shoving him, emphasizing their familiar growl. And then the younger lion simply fell over, like he had fallen asleep.

Abruptly, though, Spit pushed himself back up and sat on his legs, rousing himself. He looked about, assessing where he was. If not so sad, Spit would have been comical.

Snarl wondered how Spit would be able to take charge of the territory. The lack of other options persuaded him that Spit must stay and not follow. He doubted the younger lion understood that this whole territory now belonged to him. No matter if he knew. Snarl had done all he knew to do. Spit must find out what to do on his own.

Snarl thought that his mother must have prepared Spit, just like she had prepared him. He must trust that feeling, he decided. Spit would make his way. It was the only conclusion that Snarl could make and still leave Spit behind.

Snarl turned away from Spit, took a few steps to the edge of the canyon, looked back at his brother a last time, and flew in the air, landing a dozen feet below to the right. He bounded leap by leap down a thin, dusty, and winding trail that smelled alarmingly of coyote. He walked assured from any attempt by his brother to catch him.

A groan came low from within, a noise Snarl couldn't hold back. He sped down the path missing his mother, leaving his home, abandoning his brother, and racing toward uncertainty.

CANYON KILL

When the readily available small animals have been eaten, coyotes travel in twos to bring down larger prey. The leaders, anyway. The ones that will get to eat and live a long life end up as the leaders. They kill as a team, fill themselves as a reward, and bring food back to the den for the honor.

Howl and Teeth were such a pair. A combination of drought and too many mouths to feed forced Teeth, the pack leader, to recruit Howl to join him in the hunt for food. They belonged to a den of eight dogs, including two female adults, four males who traveled in pairs, and two pups. Two of this season's six puppies were all that remained. The others had died, one at the jaws of Teeth who had enough of the noisy, bothersome dog who did not understand that older dogs do not always want to play.

Point made.

Howl stored that information away. Pay attention to the stronger coyote's direction. One instruction is enough.

Howl considered that being the second in line to a fiercer coyote, a subordinate to Teeth, was better than being a competitor. Subservient he could be. Wary, though. Like any intelligent coyote, Howl did not sacrifice his life for the benefit of a dominant dog. Coyotes learned that survival depended upon looking out for themselves.

The coyote in Howl's pack named their canyon the Deep. That's a human translation of the place each coyote family identifies as home. Even the young learn to emit a long growl from "deep" in the esophagus.

Coyotes swallow their meat in large chunks. Larger prey is ripped apart quickly. Small game is eaten whole. This canyon had been picked clean and provided little left to harvest. The dry weather and hungry pack eradicated the regular supply of animals. They hadn't seen an elk or deer come through here in a month, much less taken one down. Hungry lions had raided their last deer kill on a mountain area to the south. They'd barely gotten a bite and left their kill with only one leg.

Rats, raccoons, mice, rabbits, birds, and squirrels were almost wiped out in their canyon, now nowhere to be found. The coyotes were left only with small berries, grass, and insects. Foraging must extend further than their few miles of canyon walls.

Hunger broadens a coyote's reach. Teeth and Howl had trekked off on a long hunt this morning, anxious to find meat. They hiked from their cave near the southern rise of another canyon, down to a blanched creek bed. Finally, they reached back toward the top of the same south side canyon wall, about three miles from their pack. That's about as far as coyotes like to travel.

Teeth smelled a lion nearby and lightly yipped to Howl. They retreated behind some rocks, sitting so still that none could tell they were there. Their gray coats resembled fallen trees, water-stained stones, or dried grass. Moving only their eyes, they peeked through a crevice between two large standing flat rocks in front of them. The crack allowed them to see through to the trail ahead, winding down the canyon.

The scent was unmistakable. Sweat and fur in the wind. Howl couldn't tell the difference between a lion that smelled of the hunt or just wandering. Didn't matter. Lions were almost always bound to be hunting.

Coyotes never toy with a cougar or mountain lion. Cats have a high success rate and will kill half of what attacks them and outrun the rest. Howl did not expect he'd be the half of a coyote duo that survives in a battle with a lion, but he calculated that Teeth would not fight unless he wanted to win.

Howl also assumed that Teeth would use him as bait. That's the way their hunting worked. One dog approached the prey, the other attacked from behind. Howl would be the coyote to scatter frightened game away from him when hunting duck or fowl, and Teeth would grab them in their escape. When hunting larger animals, Howl drew them toward Teeth, and from a hidden location, he would leap at their neck.

The same would happen now. Teeth wanted a lion kill. So, they were not hiding from this lion. Teeth had scrunched low but with paws arched. Howl sat at the left of Teeth; nearer the trail they'd just left. Teeth would push Howl into the path as soon as the lion got a whiff of coyote presence. Howl would be the bait. This was a good spot for Teeth to aim for the lion's neck.

Howl's chances were not good in this situation. He decided that a lion battle with him as the loser was not going to happen. Howl assured himself, sending sideways glances at Teeth that today was not that day. Howl could easily outrun the slower Teeth. When shoved, he was ready to ramble away.

At first, they assumed the lion was on the trail in front of them. The wind lightly blew from that direction, wafting lion scent upward. Though the coyotes sensed a lion's presence and may have heard a lion plodding along on a trail below, they didn't imagine a lion on top of them. Then, in a rush of dust and rocks from above that peppered their backs, they panicked. Both coyotes jumped like puppies in fright.

Howl spun in a remarkable 360-degree turn as he flew out of their hidden location and over the rock. He caught a face-full of pebbles just as he spied his first lion stare and hiss, all in an instant.

In the same moment, Teeth jumped straight up into the air rather than forward like Howl, unfortunately just within paw-swiping distance of his first and last encounter with an animal twice his size and more than his match. Teeth's jaw broke open, and before he could make a sound, the lion crushed his neck against the same crevice he had once been looking through.

Howl landed on his belly in front of their hiding place, legs splayed out. He scrambled to his feet in a dead run, quickly glancing back at the triumphant lion holding Teeth's limp body with one leg on his broken neck. Another leg perched on the rock where Howl had just been hiding. That was the longest stretch of animal Howl had ever seen. The lion's back two legs rose several feet up the hillside of the canyon.

How did he get so close to them?

With practiced bounces down and then back up the hillside west of the frightening sight of the lion, Howl raced away from the scene and traversed in as chaotic strides as he could make. He did not head for the den. Instead, Howl slid at the ground as he landed his paws, leaving messy, untraceable steps. He sought quick cover where there wasn't much in this forsaken place, jutting from rock to bush until he cleared the northern edge of the canyon. Howl then bolted in a sprint, running as far as he could, away from the kill zone.

Snarl ended his run at the bottom of the canyon, panting and assessing where he had come. He calmed himself by studying the parched riverbed where he stood. He could see the patterned tracks of a well-used coyote trail. The trail crossed the bottom of the canyon. Water had not been through here in months. He walked, getting back into his practiced groove of study, steady and quiet. He held his head unusually low, swaying as he went. The smell of coyote overpowered any other scents. He was in their territory but knew he was just passing through. They wouldn't bother him, he decided. Coyotes, though, were as unpredictable as any animal could be. He grew up with Spit. He knew how some could be.

There must be a hunting pair nearby, he figured. He would ignore them and let them have this place, rocky and unfriendly as it was. They would watch him, and he would keep moving.

So, caution was the plan as he surveilled the area. The canyon raised above him ahead, almost the same as he had descended. At the bottom was a relatively narrow space. He could climb up the other side and see what was beyond. That's where he could live, now. The sun's trail edge of his new home, separating his territory from Spit's.

He had hit bottom quicker than he thought and stood staring up to where he'd come, down the ridge about a mile. His keen eyes caught a glimpse of a lion almost to the top where he'd started his travel down. Too far away to tell, but it must be Spit, staring off to where he was. Good. He would stay there. He knew Spit could see him from here. Spit looked like he had something in his teeth, large.

Snarl straightened up his neck, stunned. Spit caught something on his own. Well, maybe his brother would be all right, after all.

Spit shook his head to clear the fog. Several minutes had gone by. Hunger hurt his gut. And, he'd just seen his brother jump over a cliff! It couldn't be. He stood up on all fours, took several deep breaths, and marched over to Snarl's jumping-off spot.

His breathing had calmed down. He looked over the edge. To the left, he saw two coyotes coming along a pathway. Just below, he saw where Snarl must have landed. He could see his brother heading down the path, several hundred yards away already, down and to his right. The two coyotes didn't seem to see him or his brother, but he could tell that they'd become suddenly jumpy, sniffing the air.

One of the coyotes, the bigger one, his fur coming off in patches, readying for the oncoming summer heat, yipped in a whisper to his fidgety pal. They sometimes travel in pairs, Spit remembered, assuring himself that these two were probably the only coyotes nearby. The bigger dog's teeth were constantly bared, ready to snatch at something. Spit's back raised, but he didn't flinch or blink, moving only his eyes as he studied them.

What should he do? Instead of growling to his brother or whining at his mom, he could only watch and wait.

They were on the same path as Snarl, moving steadily in his brother's direction but not looking up. His brother was far away from them. They moved too slowly if they were tracking Snarl. For some reason, they stepped off the path and climbed just a few feet below him, hiding behind some rocks. The larger one had raised his snout just before they darted into hiding. Must've smelled me, Spit thought.

The two appeared to be staring off at Snarl, though they were as still as birds in the brush. Snarl was quite a way down the path, now, almost to the bottom. The scene nearby and Snarl so far away made Spit a little dizzy. His eyes adjusted to the distances. He knew he should remain still and assess the situation before doing anything. That's what his brother would do. To steady his body on the spot he held, he slowly reset his front paws on the cliff edge, but in doing so he loosened the earth. Dirt and rocks slid from beneath his paws, landing directly on the backs of the two coyotes about six feet below him.

Both coyotes reacted in shock at the tiny avalanche of rubble and dirt bouncing off their backs. The smaller coyote flew forward, spinning in a circle, and Spit squinted and hissed at him. The bigger dog jumped straight into the air in front of Spit. Instinctively, Spit swiped his right paw at its face as it came up at him. He heard a crunch as the dog's head seemed to separate at the jawbone.

The same moment he swung at the coyote, Spit's grip on the cliff edge gave way. In what seemed like slow motion, Spit reached out with his left paw at the dog's body in mid-air. Spit used the body as a buffer as both lion and coyote landed onto the rock six feet down. His right paw timed perfectly to land on a rock to the right. His back legs remained gripped on the cliff behind him. His outstretched body must have made a splendid sight, Spit imagined.

The dog was dead under the weight of his paw. Besides the well-aimed swipe, Spit had cleanly broken its neck on the rock under his foot. He watched the other coyote run oddly all over the place, racing up and around the canyon and finally over the top to escape from him. Spit had little energy to chase after him. He enjoyed watching, though.

He jumped down to the spot behind the rocks, realizing that he'd killed himself a rare meal of coyote just in time. He was weak and starving. The dead coyote lay across the rock where his front paw had crushed the animal. Grabbing the coyote in his teeth by its broken neck, Spit walked out to the path to get a better view of the canyon below. He tried to spot his brother.

There he was, at the bottom of the canyon, looking back at him. Spit wondered if Snarl would come and share the meal he found. Snarl stood for some time, looking up. Spit hung onto the coyote, waiting for what his brother would do. And then Snarl turned and went away, up the other side of the canyon.

He couldn't be chasing that escaping coyote, Spit guessed. He wasn't sure. Plotting things and figuring out consequences weren't Spit's strength. Snarl was going the wrong way, though. Spit realized, from a place in his brain that he seldom paid attention to, that his brother must be leaving him. The long walk and his brother pushing him away replayed in his mind. Is that what Snarl was doing? He didn't fully understand what was going on. He was alone, operating entirely on guesswork. Where was his mother?

His stomach growled.

What mattered now was eating. Spit needed to feed. This much he knew.

He turned back, above the edge of the canyon, to return to familiar territory and find a quiet place to devour this dog. If Snarl was coming back, he'd better bring something of his own, Spit thought. He was sure he could eat the entire coyote all by himself.

The test of humanity grinds out on the once dusty, next muddy earth on the plains, growing corn and wheat and spices alongside nurtured herds of poultry and steerage. While in the mountains, not quite lush forests struggle to nourish deer, squirrels, and birds to feed the lions, wolves, foxes, and coyotes.

The corrupted result of allowed darkness into paradise produced this calamity of necessary harvest, barely enough to appease the survival of worldly lords managing domains measured in acres and water-formed barriers — both human and animal lords. Droughts stress the success of man and beast, and floods drown ready vegetation, whether planted or preserved.

A momentary kindness, a treasured relationship, and passionate stewardship of some sought-after balance moves between each changing arbor and inevitable season.

Between each meal, a lovely view.

Between each task, a heartened principle.

Besides everything, the divine purpose is finding its way.

Chapter Two

HOME

And I saw an angel standing in the sun, and he cried with a loud voice, saying to all the birds that did fly through the midst of heaven: Come, gather yourselves together to the great supper of God.

—APOCALYPSE 19:17

FIREFLIES

SNARL BLINKED, UNSURE WHERE he was. Lights sparkled. Was it fireflies or butterflies? He couldn't be sure. He struggled to keep his eyes open. His snout, slack and dry, lay heavy on the leafy ground. Snarl's tongue, tasteless, rubbed at his mouth, bumpy like the bark of an Elm tree. He could feel his head pounding but could not move it, nor his legs, or his back.

After some minutes, Snarl forced his head to lift, and it wobbled, falling hard to the ground. He heard purring and realized the noise was coming from him as he breathed in and out.

He pounded his head at the ground to awaken his fuzzy brain, crackling against leaves and tiny branches. Rolling life into the rest of his appendages, Snarl rocked his body to the left and the right. He rubbed the curve of his back as best he could, attempting to get some feeling along his spine. He lay on one side and now flopped with clumsy wiggles to the other.

Snarl held his head up, still only inches from the ground, stiffened his neck, and saw the lower lanky part of himself sprawled on Spruce needles and leaves that must have come from the nearby oak brush. He was lying under the source of the needles, a loping branched pine. Not a place he would have chosen, he thought. Putting his head back down, exhausted from the little effort he had already exerted, he checked out his surroundings. His eyes were slowly spinning, circling, and wobbling. He focused on another tree, a silvery Spruce. Finally, he managed to hold his eyes still.

The spot of his awakening did not look familiar. He must have picked it out but could not remember. His mouth was dry and tender.

Water. He needed water.

Breathing slowly, he tried to push energy out to his limbs, venting in and out. That seemed to work. Tingles all over assured him that his body was intact. He wanted to move. This position was not good.

Snarl sniffed the air, searching for a waft of moisture, and then cocked his ears to hear a dribble of a stream or spring nearby. Nothing. Well, not nothing. Just not a sure sound or scent of anything nearby. The blankness of sound and smells told him his hearing and sense of odors were gone.

Swallowing hurt his throat like a pinecone had gotten stuck. Pushing at his legs and arching his back, Snarl finally perched upon his side. If predators were near, they would think he was just resting. He yawned, and his face felt half numb, half tingly.

That was some sleep he was in, he thought, struggling to wake himself up. Dominant lions don't feel embarrassment, per se. They get confused at the loss of control, unfamiliar with cowering, worry that hungry animals would take advantage of weakness. Snarl stuck out his front paws and pulled up his behind. He finally sat up. As a rage of tingles ran all over him, he shifted on his front legs to control his extremities. With a mighty effort, he hopped up, sort of, and stood on all fours. He reached the ground with his snout to steady his body and then stretched out, posing a faked semblance of normalcy.

After a few moments, the tingles faded, blood flowing faster through his veins. He shook his torso like a drenched wolf would do. Snarl wanted to fully awaken but in the shaking he almost fell over.

Waking was taking too long. Lack of water, Snarl thought. He couldn't remember being without water to this extent. He reviewed what he could remember. After clearing the canyon where he left Spit, his last recollection was climbing through several dusty ridges over some unnumbered days. Maybe only one? He struggled to recall why he would be sleeping someplace strange in the middle of the day.

Oh, yes. Snarl had been walking down a broad valley. He remembered smelling deer but couldn't find them. Still cautious in new territory, he had pushed away his hunger and thirst. He was headed toward what smelled like a spring, and then . . .

He couldn't remember.

Walking, and then nothing.

Until he woke up dazed under this Pine tree.

Prance, a four-year-old doe, hid in the trees with her fawn, along with six more does and four other fawn. Their buck, a six-point, husky male named Sharp Eyes, bleated at them to stay still as he poked his head between the tall oak bush that fenced the forest from the valley view. The herd complied.

He had earlier spied two bachelor bucks loping quickly into the bush on the other side of the valley. Sharp Eye's herd had turned heads to watch the deer, too. The bucks were oddly running away, no longer tracking the herd to cull a doe away from Sharp Eye. They had moved fast, deliberately, either from being chased or from something they saw.

At the unknown danger, Sharp Eye's herd instantly hurried behind trees and bush in practiced fashion. They instinctively froze, still as bark. A few moments later, Prance saw a lion slowly walking out from the trees on the lower side of the valley.

The lion did not move like others she had seen. Lions don't walk openly with so many deer about. His tongue hung low. Shouldn't he be chasing after the two bucks there just ahead of him, into the woods?

Her fawn leaned against Prance's flank behind a set of low-branched long-needle pines. Prance hissed at her youngster to be still. She could see over Sharp Eyes backside into the valley, through a dotted opening in the oak brush.

Then, in a snap of sound the lion flew backward. His legs flung up, and his body made a cracking noise, like a broken branch. The downed lion dropped near the creek. Prance reckoned so because the stream traveled right down the center of the valley. She heard only a popping sound, and then the animal crumpled. How did he make that noise as he fell, she wondered?

Prance's body twitched. The regal buck did, too, like he does at every sound, but more so at this slapped noise. He slowly stepped out from behind the oak before him and focused on where the lion fell.

Maybe the lion was hiding, Prance thought, watching the attentive buck. The dangerous beast would be crawling, now, toward them. There! She could see what might be the lion's back but she wasn't sure. Those could just be some rocks. She looked over to Sharp Eyes. He must have thought the same thing because he turned on his back legs, pivoted and hopped quickly away, deeper into the forest. The other doe and fawns immediately followed. Prance aimed to follow, too, but turned her head to check one more time.

Prance lived on high alert. More cautious than the others, having forfeited a half-grown fawn to a lion some time back, a misfortune foisted upon a mothering doe by hungry predators and only a moment's inattention. The lesson to double-check had been learned from tragedy.

The lion, or rock pile, hadn't moved. Prance's fawn leaned on her mother's flank, even as they both jumped after the others. The careful mother doe was not clear on the lion's situation but needed to keep up. She ran, and her fawn bounced off and on against the doe's belly as she felt her mother's urgency, staying close, as she had been taught.

WALKING EAGLE

Walking Eagle McDermott was a retired forest ranger. He worked for the Clayhall family and managed their mountain ranch and rangeland. "What's the job?" he'd asked Clayhall.

"Keep an eye on things."

That aptly summed up McDermott's daily tasks. The ranch operations included no animals, like cattle or sheep. Just those that wandered the property — migrant wildlife and wildlife residents. Not an actual ranch, really.

McDermott had retired early, after just twenty years with the Forest Service. He wanted to remain on wild land, and Clayhall's parcel fit the bill.

The retired ranger wished the Fish and Game Department had more money for research. Now a private citizen, McDermott went mostly by his Ute name, Walking Eagle. He kept active contact with folks he'd known for years. That's how he acquired anesthetic darts from the University of Colorado, a necessary tool for the tracking/marking task Walking Eagle performed for decades. Fish and Game had a small budget to gather the necessary data, relying mostly on volunteers. Data on monitoring the counts and health of mountain lions, that is.

Most folks just counted lions, but Walking Eagle liked to keep up with the health of the animals, too. The university had a great program going, keeping annual blood work on a large set of lions throughout the state. They learned a lot from studying the lions — diseases, nutrition, and wear on the lion's bodies.

The university funding for the mountain lion study, however, was also paltry. Darts weren't especially expensive, but the data gathering, analysis, and blood tests program cost a pretty penny. The university only provided anesthesia and syringes for the number of blood tests they could afford.

Though retired from the forest service, Walking Eagle still participated in the annual lion counts for this region of Colorado. Annually, he would dart the local, dominating lions, including those on the Clayhall ranch, and take some blood samples for the folks at the university to study. He'd done so today. Well, he'd shot the dart.

Walking Eagle didn't get to take a blood sample because the mountain lion he darted was new to the area. His eyesight was not the same as when he was younger. Up close, he discovered that this cougar was not a local lion.

This cougar was young, certainly outside his pride's territory. McDermott knew the young offspring from the females who lived in the areas around the Clayhall ranch. This male was not one of them. Wrong coloring, a rare white set of hair strands above one eye. He didn't take a blood sample because he didn't have time to register the animal. Walking Eagle hit the lion in the neck, which could be fatal. Attention needed to address the lion's chances at survival.

This lion darting was not a typical shoot. Walking Eagle was forced to dart under duress. Darting was better than killing, though.

This wasn't hunting season. Well, not technically. Walking Eagle certainly didn't have the separate license for a late winter/early spring harvest that the state enacted just a few days ago. Even if he had a rifle, shooting in defense, there would be a ton of paperwork to fill out. All in all, good that he had the dart. Unfortunately, no blood samples for the university.

The lion surprised him. Walking Eagle McDermott was sitting low in a stream between some rocks on the Clayhall Ranch valley floor. Waiting for a local lion, he was also carefully eyeing the path of a bear several hundred yards above him. The wind was coming from the top of the hill but changed erratically. Downwind east for a while, and then west, upwind. Walking Eagle would soon have to leave the area for his truck because the bear would smell him. Never know what a bear will do.

Walking Eagle didn't pursue lions like serious hunters, using packs of hounds. The dogs were safer to use and much better at treeing a lion. Darting a lion in a tree is easier. Taking care of trained hunting dogs exhausted him. Clayhall's nephew had one, a Bluetick coonhound. Part Cur, he met the clever dog a month ago. Walking Eagle's lone pup was a housebound loud terrier glued to the arms of his wife and daughter. He preferred the solo challenge of waiting for the wild animals to come to him.

Too old to take care of a couple of high-maintenance hunting dogs meant his experience mattered even more. He expected a local lion might be passing this way because it was just before dawn.

Walking Eagle might have known right away, with a younger man's eyesight, that this lion was a stranger. It was not among any on the cat inventory list for the ranch's tagged lions.

Mr. Clayhall was a good man to let animals range freely on his spread. Walking Eagle liked the ranchman, mostly because he let the forest ranger act more like a game warden than a cowboy. He quit forestry for health reasons. Thinking he'd move over to Colorado Fish and Wildlife Conservation, McDermott landed this job, a private caretaker getting to do both forest and wildlife work. Not much stress. No bureaucracy. A boss dependent upon him, rather than the other way around. Home every night.

"Thank you, Jesus," he said, crouching between a far off bear and an ambling cougar.

Walking Eagle knew the tracks and behaviors of all the large animals on the ranch. This lion was very quiet, slow-moving. He wasn't stalking, just traveling. The lion walked tall with little swagger, plodding with his head on a steady, rocking swivel. Rather than let the lion discover him hiding so near, Walking Eagle took the shot.

The noise from the dart gun made a popping, then slight whizzing sound. The anesthetic usually takes several minutes to stop an animal as big as a lion. It was a clean shot, though, right into the lion's neck. The animal dropped immediately.

"Wow," thought Walking Eagle. The dart must have hit the carotid artery. He waited to be sure the lion was down. A few minutes later, he made his way to the body, finally assured the cougar was out cold.

It was young, not familiar to him.

Because of the bear, Walking Eagle tied and covered the lion and prepared to get him out of the valley. The vulnerable animal would need a safe place to recover before he awakened. No sense creating a forest conflict if he could help it.

Walking Eagle's truck was just behind the trees on the mountain road, a long walk. He hurried to it, one eye up the valley. He couldn't see the bear anywhere. Once in the truck, he hastily backed it over to the lion, lowered the tailgate, and loaded him up.

He drove back over to the road, then took it all the way to the top of the valley. He stopped where he'd parked many times before to watch animals above the edge of the valley. It was not far, 100 yards or so, from the source of the valley's spring.

He hoped that the lion would wake up before the bear or any other animals arrived. His truck's presence usually sent most predators running off. This high up the hill would be safer. He lifted the lion and set him down on a soft patch of undergrowth near a large tree. He got back in his vehicle and drove as far away as he could, still able to watch, just in case some predator came upon the unconscious lion.

Once settled into his truck, safely away and watching the still body of the sleeping cougar, Walking Eagle began to worry. The youngster would be unusually thirsty when he awoke, especially with the drug going so quickly to his brain. Since he shot the lion near the lower valley's creek, he hoped the lion had found water recently.

If not, he'd indeed find the upstream portion of the creek from here.

He rubbed his gloved hands around the steering wheel, wondering what else he should do. The headspring that sourced the valley's creek was hidden from Walking Eagle's view. He moved his truck backward, further into some brush.

He got comfortable and cranked his seat lower to stretch out. In a few minutes, his periodic peeks at the lion came less often. He fell into a deep sleep.

BEAR

Hair, an aged brown bear, had been sitting at the head of his stream, near the top end of a long valley. He was upset, slapping foam away from the rocks. Something seemed wrong with the water.

Nothing was wrong with the water, though.

Hair was usually a slow-moving, careful bear. Not now. Water flew in all directions as he splashed at foam in the stream. It's the water, he thought. Bear was certain. And he was wrong.

The water was not the problem.

Hair could not connect the rotting fish waste he piled up at the stream's source and the lack of insects to break down the waste. He had no problem doing this at other points in the stream. At the spring head, though, a mixed dose of various mineral gases seeps out of deep water. Some of those gases are dangerous. Insects don't hang around gaseous air.

Hair didn't know about toxic mineral gases in springheads. Hair was not a biologist nor a chemist. He was a gatherer of food and an eager consumer of the food he gathered. All he could see were the results — dirty, stinky foam. The foam disturbed his eating pleasure.

Bears like clean water, the kind flowing in streams and creeks. The foam wasn't there before, and now it was. Hair wanted the water fixed.

Spring gas does not affect large animals like Hair unless they hold their noses to it for long periods. Why would they ever do that?

Insects and smaller animals almost always stay away from a stream's headwater gurgling up from deep below. Because they are small, the gas can overpower them. Consequently, the garbage from Hair's meals had piled up over the last few weeks. No other animals came by, nor did any insects. At other stream locations, insects and other living things cleaned up behind him. He never noticed before that his messes needed cleaning, nor did he realize the junk he created was the problem behind the water's foam.

Hair had come to enjoy his berries, trout, and seeds while sitting quietly by the moving water of the stream. He took a liking to his latest spot, where the water bubbled out of the ground. He enjoyed his meals, his sitting places, and his clean water.

No one bothered bears while they ate. No one bothered walking bears or sleeping bears either. Hair, however, was very bothered. A rotting smell that he didn't like remained hanging in the air.

Green algae had formed to do the job of breaking down Hair's waste. Algae take weeks to grow. Eventually, vast amounts of algae developed upon the rotting trash compounding the stench of fish carcasses and half-eaten plant life the bear had deposited there. Hair didn't know about the similar jobs that algae and insects perform.

Maybe he would have known if someone had told him.

Smacking at the growing greenish bubbles ringing the rocks about his newfound dining area, Hair became more and more enraged. He wanted to make the foam go away, but it wouldn't. He grumbled at the green, slimy water, but it wouldn't clear up. He sniffed the air and did not like the smell. He ran over the rocks several times, pounded at the water, and made quite a mess of his pleasant spot. He kicked his pile of smelly trash in every direction. His rage damaged the spring's decades of harmonious granite and volcanic rock and tore up all the plant life. In a matter of minutes, he destroyed his delightful meal-eating setting.

The spring continued unabated and delivered the underground water randomly in a muddy mess. Water spouted in every direction. As it spread, a second stream path formed anew, somewhat parallel to the existing creek. It rejoined the old creek about 50 yards into the valley.

Still worked up over the inconsiderate grass-colored bubbles, Hair felt his stomach growl. His own internal gases were building up, which meant he needed to relieve himself. Against a calm bear's better judgment and acting unsuitably rash, Hair stopped where he stood and pooped. Half his feces joined in the flowing water pathway down the new creek, bobbing and weaving through rocks.

The trail of events had Hair flummoxed. He was totally confused by his own behavior. He moved away from the headwater and reviewed the scene. In fact, the spring gases may have contributed to Hair's behavior. No scientists were around to assess that possibility.

The greenish bubbles and sticky algae had finally floated away, but the pleasant dining area was no more. The stream poured everywhere. The smell now seemed worse.

Hair loped downstream to get away from there, still quite miffed at the unfortunate state of his usually enjoyable mealtime. He made a promise to never go up to that spot again. By the time he had calmed down to his regular slow ramble along the stream, Hair paused and sniffed at the creek several hundred yards later. It finally smelled right.

The lumbering bear, and his antics, however, spooked a family of prairie dogs. When the bear went quiet, they left their burrow near the stream for a secondary hole they'd made further toward the trees. The prairie dogs, coincidentally, rustled up a group of game hens as they sped by them. The bear did not notice the skittering prairie dogs or the flustered, frightened game hens.

The wind shifted from upwind, blowing instead from the creek's stream head down into the valley. Hair stood on his hind legs, and the rotting scent overwhelmed him once more. His keen nose could only conclude that the smell had now taken over the entire valley. That meant, in his limited calculus, that the valley was ruined.

Again, the smell was not from the water, but Hair did not know that.

Hair growled at the stream in a returning rage and ran through it, splashing and thrashing rocks. He systematically battered the creek all the way back up to the head of the valley. The trip upstream always took longer than walking downstream, but Hair was busy creating havoc as he went.

The long wet hair on his body whipped in synch with his whirlwind swing at everything in his wake. He pummeled at the stream waters, rock formations, lovely grass bundles, and scenic hanging branches within his reach. Rocks, limbs, plants, and dirt flew everywhere as he battled the water and smell. He intended to obliterate the creek, crashing onward and upward, back to where the waters first bubbled. Hair was on a rage-filled mission.

A Peregrine falcon named Pikes Beak circled high in the air. He was slowly navigating up and down the stretched valley below him, waiting for prey, low flying juvenile hawks, scurrying rodents, or head-bobbing robins. Anything, really.

A distraction came from the top of the valley. The falcon tracked a bear crashing down the valley's creek, obviously upset and angry. He kept bounding down into the broad section of the valley, splashing and leaping as he went.

Abruptly, the bear stopped and began rocking on his four limbs, breathing hard. He lifted his snout and smelled the air. The heat from the bear's resting body rippled in the air, all the way up to Pikes Beak. He flew closer.

The bear shook, stood up and growled. More like a roar. The falcon was not in any danger but turned both wings to head higher anyway.

Now the bear was running back up the valley! Something serious was going on. Pikes Beak pursued the bear from a distance, water spray and debris flying as the bear rumbled, very angry about something.

The bear was not helping the falcon's hunt, clamoring about like that, but Pikes Beak was far too curious to leave. Besides, maybe the raging animal would scare out some small bird that he could snare from the air.

He circled, waiting and watching.

There! Prairie dogs skittered into the tall grass, startled by the bear. Oh! Some fat, juicy game hens had decided to show themselves as the rodents ran by them. Perfect! But the scattering movements were chaotic. Too much commotion. Pikes Beak couldn't focus on one target. His eyes jumped about, confused by each animal's maneuvering. He hesitated an instant too long, and everything stopped. The animals were suddenly gone in the flickering grass, and probably back underground. Pikes Beak couldn't pinpoint any of them. He flew in a slow climbing circle, hoping to catch a glimpse of still feathers or twitching hair. One of them was sure to wiggle or turn.

Concentrated on rampant destruction, Hair eventually arrived at the original point of his raging attack on the waters. He stopped at the spring-head on all fours and pounded hard at the mud in the middle of his previous lovely area. He then shook water, soil, and sundry other materials attached to his matted body in a rotating fury.

Hair stretched up on his hind legs to growl away the smell. He mustered up an intense store of energy and lifted his arms in a murderous pose ... but, there, directly in front of Hair, stood a mountain lion. Posed in stark contrast to the bear, less than one quarter Hair's size, the lion stood just up the slope, only a dozen feet away from the head of the spring.

Hair forgot his rage, the stink, the foam, and his ruined mealtime. He stood dripping, the steam of an overheated bear floating off his shimmering, drenched, and muddy body. In an instant, his heaving shoulders went rigid.

Hair stared, still as a bear knew he must be. As still as a bear in the face of a lion needed to be, that is.

The lion was not as big as some he had seen, but this lion held a gaze on Hair that he'd never experienced before. The cat's large, steely eyes did not move. Not a flicker of his tail, either.

Hair considered for a moment that he should follow through with that roar he had already been poised to make. He was upright and must indeed present an incredible image for the lion to see. So, Hair shook with all his strength and growled a bellow that could be heard throughout the valley.

The trees flickered, birds flew, and even the scant clouds appeared to react. The lion, however, didn't move a muscle. Not a twitch. It stood, apparently unfazed, staring at the bear.

Recognizing his awkward position of belly open and standing perilously in the mud, the old bear dropped to all fours. He made a point to splash hard when he landed, expecting some reaction from the lion. But, again, nothing.

The bear's snout moved in as menacing an expression as he could show while he kept his head still. He focused on the amazingly calm lion. Seconds passed without effect.

In a rushed calculation of the situation, the bear decided to let the lion have this spot if he wanted it. He abandoned this place for a host of reasons. A confusing day that went bad with green foam, the wrong stink, a treacherous creek, and this immovable cougar. Besides, the one-mile demolition hike uphill had spent his energy's reserves.

Hair acted as if nothing at all had taken place. He ignored the lion completely, turned, and walked down the stream into the valley. The smell returned periodically. Hair growled at it for good measure each time he picked up that awful scent. Here and there, he kicked away rocks in the stream out of spite.

Halfway down the valley and roaming far-off the creek to the right, Hair re-startled that small group of game hens that had reeled earlier from the scurrying prairie dogs. The bear watched them grouped tightly together flickering in the sun. Then in a flash, the hens fluttered their wings, and they seemed to be flying apart. The bear, wide-eyed, was shocked at them flopping around in a tornado of feathers.

After that surprise, Hair was unnerved again. A dark, large bird exited the hen pile and flew straight up, gripping floppy, feathery bodies in its feet.

More oddity. More confusion and weird behavior.

Hair decided to keep going and leave this blighted and foul-smelling place to the lion and the weird animals that now inhabited the valley. He never looked back, not wanting to give the lion any sense that he feared him.

The water, he was sure, was broken here, anyway.

After gathering his senses and feeling his legs somewhat steady beneath him, Snarl set out after the smell of the creek he remembered following just a few hours ago. Or was it longer? He would concentrate more this time and stay awake and more aware, he decided.

The smell he found, however, was not of water but something rancid. Snarl's scent interpretation reminded him of an old, abandoned kill, but more fragrances were involved. Mixed up smells. Fish and poorly deteriorating, maybe even swampy plant life. Mostly grass, maybe? Uneaten, perhaps. Rotten for sure.

The scent came from close by. Snarl was surprised at how long it took to smell unless it was just unleashed from something. His sense of smell had been affected by his deep sleep. Whiffs, fumes, and forest scents were now fully awakened, and Snarl processed them all.

Recovering in bits and pieces, Snarl moved, quickening his pace to find out what was there and to re-orient all his senses. As he headed up the hill, following the smells, he spied the hidden flanks of two deer, over to his left, on a lower hillside in the brush. They were watching him, quietly frozen as he walked by. His eyesight had come back, too. That was good. He pretended to ignore them.

Normally, Snarl would have picked up their scent before they noticed him, but he had trouble separating out their smell from that coming over the top of the hill in front of him. He could tell that they were young deer, males. Their hide sweat gave off a particular scent. The air, though, was filled with many conflicting and sour smells. He marked the place in his visual memory to register two bucks hiding. Snarl then trod on at the same pace toward his investigation, letting the deer think he had not seen them.

He was very close to a hilltop when he noticed a strange set of two wide animal trails crossing in front of him. Snarl had run into this phenomenon before. The tracks made no sense because they were so wide, straight, and evenly furrowed. Not like the padding of any animal he knew. He turned and followed the dual trails. Snarl stopped near the hilltop because the dirt paths now headed away from the top of the hill where the scent of water and stink might be.

He paused. The tracks were familiar where Snarl had woken up under the spruce. Similar, newer, dual channels were near that spot. Not as pronounced as these. No time for that now, he thought. He turned away from the broad, worn dual tracks and walked to the top. He needed to drink.

Rank aromas filled the air just over the hill. A mist of dirt and floating rot hung about the place. Sparkly, tiny particles of dead plants and fetid bits of meat filled the space above the ground. Fish, plants and maybe bear, Snarl decided, as he took in each of the scents. He stood dumbstruck at the hilltop.

An uneasy quiet, mixed with the noisy-looking scene, cautioned Snarl. Whatever caused this ruckus might be lurking nearby. He couldn't see any animals, certainly nothing monstrous enough to create what hung in the air. He stalked into the reeking mist.

Indeed, this was a battle zone. Combat had taken place, that's for sure, but the only fatalities appeared to be fish and plants. Impossible, he thought. What would they be fighting over? Did plants here battle with fish?

This new territory presented wonders beyond his imagination. Snarl focused again on his original goal, from when he had awoken in a strange place. Water.

He stepped forward and saw water bubbling ahead amid the devastation. Lightly stepping forward, he sensed danger, but he could not detect any living foe. He stepped lightly for two reasons. First, he was still weak. Secondly, a predator may be nearby.

As he approached the water coming straight out of the ground, similar to some larger springs he had seen before, he thought perhaps the water had done all this.

Quickly Snarl stepped back, assessing how that could be possible. Finally, he saw a fixed set of paw prints. Bear. He looked around and saw a eroded pile of large scat dumping, partly spread by flowing water. He did not see any parts of a bear torn up in what must have been a fierce fight. The tracks of the bear, a big one, were scattered in an almost crazy fashion. They all looked the same, but Snarl assumed that two bears must have fought here.

The bear scat was totally out of place. Most confusing, Snarl thought to himself. No bear fur from a fight. No blood. One large pile of bear scat right near the water.

He felt woozy because he still hadn't gotten water. Snarl cautiously stepped toward the source of the water, a bubbly spring pushing through mud. He shifted above the bubbling in case the water contained a dangerous occupant. Maybe that's what happened to the bear.

As he approached the stream head from above, his diligence paid off. One last review of the area revealed a loping bear racing up the creek. He was a hundred yards down the valley but charging fast. Not only rushing but flinging rocks, dirt, plants and splashing through the stream with an incredible display of anger and outrage. Snarl could already hear the bear's labored breathing. The animal was exerting an enormous amount of energy.

This must be the winning bear returning to claim the water? Or returning to attack something in water once again. More likely, he finally thought . . . the bear was coming to attack him.

Checking his position, Snarl estimated that the bear would be upon him in only a few seconds. Lions don't measure time in seconds. They estimate by the beats of their heart or the pounding of blood through their head. It's a nascent, rudimentary comparison of time and distance. He'd learned this relatively young.

Snarl was weak and extremely thirsty. He could not escape this creature. Maybe the bear hadn't yet noticed him. Slowly, he tried to back up further from the spring but his body would not cooperate. It took everything he had just to remain standing.

Snarl regretted not getting a drink of water. The bear was his primary problem, so he dared not take his eyes off the beast. Snarl remained still as he called up the last of his reserves.

The bear stopped just a few dozen feet in front of him. Snarl didn't let his tail move off the ground because it helped brace him upright. The bear had not yet looked at him. In the same odd pose of prairie dog, a colossal one at that, the bear popped up, standing on his hind legs with his arms at his side. It looked to his left, down the valley. The mightiest gesture of an animal Snarl had ever seen. The picture of this scene would forever remain in his memory banks. Snarl didn't move a whisker.

The mountain lion was correct. When the bear turned back to look at the stream his head stopped abruptly. Snarl's presence surprised him. He stood just below the springhead, Snarl uphill above. That placed the bear and the lion eye to eye. Snarl stood his ground. It was all he could do.

Snarl stared into the bear's eyes, wondering what that big old animal was thinking. Would he attack?

Only a moment or two went by and the bear roared, lifting his head high and his arms higher. Snarl watched in awe, grateful he did not faint. He'd never heard any noise like that up close. Snarl could feel the breath of the bear's roar over his body. Incredible!

Eventually, the roaring stopped, and Snarl watched the bear look at him over his large black snout. Since Snarl had not reacted to the roar, maybe the bear was confused. In another circumstance, the lion would probably have run at first sight of him but he was in a fragile state. Running would not be good. He wasn't even sure if he could run at all, much less outrun a beast like this.

Then, in another startling move, the bear dropped to the ground on all fours with great emphasis. Perhaps the bear was going to charge. Snarl knew he had little strength to defend himself, so he thought it best to preserve every ounce of energy he had. When he comes, Snarl decided, he'd dive at the last instant for the bear's throat. That was his only hope.

The bear didn't charge. He waggled his snout for a bit and turned away. Snarl was surprised and dizzy. He was about to crumble. His legs started shaking.

Before the bear realized Snarl's weakness, he had walked away. Snarl fell forward, struggled to the spring, and began lapping away at the bubbling water. It was fantastic. And not a second left to wait. He lay on his belly, his arms by his sides, lightly licking at the water, immersing his snout. All the while, he watched the bear wander back down the valley.

Snarl began fading into sleep, still very weak yet thankful for the cool water. He watched the bear and, far off, saw a falcon dive for the bear's head. But, it missed, appearing to crash into an explosion of feathers off to the right.

An astonishing place, Snarl thought. The strangest sights, smells, hunting behaviors, water antics, and animal behavior that he'd ever experienced. This place was nothing like home.

With his face in the bubbling water, Snarl felt his body go loose. He felt so tired. The water rushing over his nose felt good. He couldn't move his front paws. Soon, he wasn't able to lift his head out of the water or even move his tongue. His eyes could see, but nothing else was in control. The water covered his mouth and nose. He closed his eyes and relaxed.

Snarl began to dream, not something he'd ever imagined before and not something he would really describe as a dream. All thought to Snarl was the same, whether awake or asleep. He didn't know the difference. If you could explain to him what a dream is, though, he would nod in agreement that this must be dreaming.

In his dream, water filled his lungs as he tried to breathe, but there wasn't anything he could do. He knew he must back out of the water, but his body wouldn't respond. Darkness, the one with rash thoughts, took over. It told him to swallow the spring. He resisted because the idea didn't sound correct. He waited instead for another thought to come.

Suddenly, he felt his legs move on their own. They took charge and dragged his body away from the water. His legs pulled him backward, enough for his face to lift out of the water. Free from the water, his legs let go.

He had remained calm, confident in his ability to wait.

He had waited out the urge to kill his brother.

He had waited out the bear.

He had waited out the killing water.

Lying downhill, Snarl felt the water slowly pour out of his body. His breathing started again.

Snarl felt satisfied, pleased with everything that had happened to him. He didn't move. He relished the power of waiting.

As a grateful gesture, Snarl lifted his tail and swatted his legs, thanking them for a better idea.

Pikes Beak carried two-game hens in his talons, flying along the tree-tops to the upward edge of the valley. That was an extraordinary grab he made on those birds, he thought to himself. After the bear went back down the valley again, his waddling romping, less wild but still lively, rustled up the game hens again.

Pikes Beak dove for them, speeding like a dark feathery lightning bolt. The falcon was in and out before the bear even knew what had happened.

As he carried his meal near the valley top, on his way back to his nest in the red rocks, Pikes Beak saw that the water flowed all over the place up at the springhead. He angled his wings, gliding in a circle to check out what happened.

A considerable brawl had taken place, a mayhem of mud covered the rocks and the grass. The bear must have tussled with another formidable animal because the lumbering fellow left empty-handed, loping back down the valley.

The falcon swung low and then abruptly turned back into the treetops, tightening his grip. Below, a lion lay flat on the ground, head poked directly into the bubbling springhead. Ah, maybe the bear had killed it. It did not look maimed, though. Perhaps the lion was faking, preparing to leap at the curious falcon.

Then, the shadow of a human appeared over the lion, and a man stepped out from the trees and stood behind the lion. Pikes Beak wisely chose to exit into the trees.

Too much activity, he thought. Without further distractions, he head-ed for his hole in the red rock cliffs farther into the mountains. He gripped the game hens tighter, craned his neck for speed, steeling his eyes in a fur-row at his carelessness. Pikes Beak crested his wings into the wind, shouting caws at invisible predators that may think he wasn't at the ready. While the springhead commotion was interesting, Pikes Beak might have dropped his meal to observe a curiosity.

Hidden predators mixed with odd distractions make for a dangerous hunting adventure.

The trash inside Walking Eagle's truck included hamburger wrappings, not quite empty bags of chips, crushed root beer cans, and at least one spilled milkshake. The smell woke him up.

The lion was gone, aroused when Walking Eagle had fallen asleep. Too bad, thought Walking Eagle. He'd missed him. Thankfully, the lion must have recovered.

Looking inside his truck, Walking Eagle moaned, disgusted at the debris. He stepped outside to make sure his lift gate was up. After quietly shutting his door, he sniffed. The odor was strong, like the city dump. Those trash smells were not coming from his truck.

The retired ranger scratched his chin and shifted from worry about the lion to worry about the rancid air. He could smell the lion's residue on his gloves. Distinctive scent.

The awakened lion must have walked right by him, following the old ranch road he had driven away from the spruce tree. The smell was coming from the direction of the creek. If the lion headed up and over the hilltop to the springhead, it might still be there.

Walking carefully, Walking Eagle spied the lion standing at the springhead. He froze, hiding behind a tree. He was at a safe distance, but it would be tricky getting back to the truck if the lion saw him.

The lion stood still. Had it already taken a drink? Walking Eagle wondered what was bothering the animal. The lion seemed to be staring down the valley.

That's when Walking Eagle saw a bear running up the creek at the lion. Walking Eagle knew it was probably better to retreat, but he couldn't stop watching what would happen. The scene that followed was more than surprising.

In a few seconds, the bear challenged the lion in a standing position and roared aggressively. Dropping to all fours, the bear seemed poised to attack, like a defensive lineman on a football team. Walking Eagle knew that stance. He'd played football in high school, not 20 miles away in Palmer Lake.

The lion, though, stood still as a statue and stared down the bear. If only Walking Eagle had sense enough to video this, he thought. His phone was on the dash.

Then, cool as a cucumber, the bear turned and left.

Walking Eagle shook his head at the site and thought now would be an excellent time to run back to the truck. Before he turned, the lion wavered and then stumbled forward. It fell into the spot where the spring water came out. The lion's movements didn't look right.

The odors already in the air were coming from that spring, Walking Eagle sensed. He slowly backed away and ran to the truck, looking back for the lion, or maybe the bear traversing from another direction.

He grabbed his shotgun from the back window seat. It was not a dart gun that he selected this time. He then crept back to see what had happened to the lion. As he approached, he saw the lion, still, lying there, his head immersed in the water.

Walking Eagle moved a little faster, worried that the lion had either succumbed again to the anesthetic he had given him in the dart. He might be drowning. He got a little closer, and flying out of his left, he saw a falcon swoop by and then away.

The falcon was already carrying something in his feet. Walking Eagle was impressed by the falcon's audacity to consider attacking this lion. The forest ranger in him kicked back into gear, and he cocked the shotgun, ready if needed.

He was too close to actually use it. He tapped the lion's rear legs, splayed out like he was stretched in prayer or something. His snout was covered entirely by the water. Danged if that lion hadn't fainted, he whispered out loud.

The lion didn't respond.

Carefully, Walking Eagle uncocked, then put down his shotgun and squatted behind the lion. He slowly wrapped his hands just above the back paws. Boy, these lion paws are sure large, he thought, as he tested the lion's consciousness. Again, no response from the lion.

He thought it was too late, but out of respect for the lion, Walking Eagle pulled at the lion and dragged him until his face and snout were out of the water.

"Never done that before," he said, louder.

Reaching down for his gun, he walked backward for a bit. He then took off running to his truck, looking over his shoulder every now and then to be sure the lion wasn't awake suddenly and chasing after him.

He was breathing hard when he finally got back in the truck, still clutching the gun in his hands. "Wow," he kept muttering. "Wow." Over and over.

He started the truck and drove higher up the road where he could make out the lion's position. He stayed there watching the lion for 10 minutes or so. No movement from the courageous animal. A sadness came over him, as he thought that the lion may have died because of his good intentions gone awry. Both Walking Eagle and the lion's good intentions, he thought.

Just as he was about to exit the vehicle and retrieve the seeming dead lion, he saw its tail move. It flapped up into the air and against his back legs.

OK, maybe he'll be alright.

The smell from the mess in his truck reminded Walking Eagle that his presence included the hamburger wrappers on the floor. He decided he'd best get out of here before the lion woke up. That poor animal might be thoroughly ruined by something else that an old forest ranger might do.

Even one with good intentions.

The seasons, the rising sun, and the axial motion of stars above repeat toward a purpose. Don't they? We assume a beginning took place. Celestial placements likely induced ensuing gravity. Energy sparked everything in the universe to introduce time. Or was it the rattling of power that forced time upon an already perfect system?

A frolicking band of jungles, deserts, and waters clothe the planet earth, capped at two ends by ice on a single planet among more solar systems than history can count. We've only just discovered they may not go on forever.

There is no forever for anything we can see. What then at the necessary end? Creation and all of its created thoughts and calculations amount to guesses. A creator, many of us conclude, listens, watches, and even communicates with us. Such a creator solves the eternal, actual forever conundrum.

Listening, in the animal understanding of how any of us hear, can be observed. So, we extend our belief that God too listens, understands, and speaks.

The human ear in consort with its other senses, including transcendent abilities, is similar in the animal world. It seems so. The animals, then, can hear God's voice. If God can speak, then we can be assured of his presence. Can we also hear revelation from God? Even his intervention? Does God reach all of creation like he can reach us?

This is what we chew on.

Chapter Three

FAMILY

The wolves and the lambs feed together, and the lion shall eat straw like the ox; but the serpent [shall eat] earth as bread. They shall not hurt or maltreat each other on the holy mountain . . .

—ISAIAH 65:25

TUFT

CLAW HUDDLED WITH HER newborn kittens. She had not left them alone for long. They fed on her body constantly. She found mice yesterday and a rabbit the day before. So, she was strong. Her new home was an abandoned den. She could stay here until they were larger.

She licked them, and they rolled closer to her. Their warm and soft bodies were already changing. Claw felt bones between her teeth as she drew them nearer. This new place fit them well. She must claim the land if that is possible. She decided to investigate the canyon later. For now, she would rest.

Within many hundred large, ridged ravines flowing into the western lands from the Rocky Mountain Range lived separate lions securing their territory. Two families of migrating cougars contemplated home in the same already populated ravine — Claw with her cubs and the lone Snarl. The resident lion family consisted of one mother lion and her two grown cubs.

Tuft, the ravine's only resident female cub, lacked fundamental territory defenses or hunting skills. She was about to be the only local lion due to unfortunate circumstances.

Racing into her home's canyon at the lower end of the ravine, Tuft scrambled for a safe place to hide. The frantic cub ran just ahead of what she thought was a pack of snarling wolves.

The day would move from bad to worse. Her problems had started the night before.

Tuft, with her brother and their mother, lived together under a craggy granite ledge. The space could house three adult-sized lions without any problem. They spent the days on warm rocks that looked over much of the ravine's length which they claimed as their own. The view allowed a panoramic scan from the upper end of the canyon and east toward flatlands.

Tuft's brother was deep into a daytime nap on his favorite rock still digesting last night's meal. He had consumed almost everything, not letting either Tuft or her mother eat. Circumstances leading Tuft to flee for her life involved an accident on a hunt and a mistaken identity.

On the previous evening, Tuft's kin successfully separated a young doe from its buck. The mother distracted the aggressive buck while Tuft joined her brother in cornering the doe.

The hunt went as planned. The three of them could overcome just about any sized buck. This buck, however, had deftly kicked Tuft's mother in the head during the scuffle. Dismissing the pain, she managed to divert the charging deer so her offspring could take down the doe. The tactic worked. After her brother grabbed the doe by its now broken neck and ran off, Tuft and her mother followed him and left the hard-breathing buck behind.

The kick, however, had done severe damage to Tuft's mother. She tripped and fell several times on their escape and finally collapsed back at their den. Tuft's brother, much larger than the mother, took advantage of the head injury. He refused to share the deer. Stinginess had become a recent, disappointing pattern. Weakened by the fight, the mother could not restrain her much stronger son from hoarding the kill.

After a feeble attempt at control, the mother gave up. She was shaky and unable to control her balance. He initially pushed her away with intimidating growls and then boldly knocked her a fair distance with a sharp swing of his butt. She struggled to get up, then left the den, stumbling away. Tuft watched her fall, and crawl, and rise again several times as she headed toward the small creek that ran the length of the ravine. The stream was not far from either their winter or summer spot. Her mother's exit direction made sense — just a short walk to the rise at the top of the ravine to catch the stream's beginnings or a safe traipse through the brush to any spot lower in the creek.

Whenever wounded, the lions headed for the stream. Anyplace the water traveled down the valley was good, except the larger openings in the gorge. Tuft assumed her mother would gather her strength there.

Tuft's brother dragged the kill to a spot just below their sleeping area, where he usually spent his day sunning in the warmth. During that night, Tuft intermittently fought him to get something to eat. After each failed attempt, she cried out to her mother. She never came to help. Her brother overpowered her. He had even bit her.

Tuft didn't sleep between struggles to snatch a part of the kill. As dawn crept into the day, she was exhausted and dizzy. Tuft decided to retrieve her mother who had still not come back to the den. Maybe the two of them could wrest the kill from her selfish brother, if anything remained that is.

She followed the path to the creek her mother had taken the evening before. After the trek to the stream, she walked a few hundred yards until she found her mother lying under a stretch of Kinnikinnick growth. Her body lay surprisingly still, ribs showing no up and down from her breathing. Tuft nudged her with her nose but got no reaction.

Tuft picked up confusing smells — lion, fox, but predominantly decay. The stench from her mother's body was overwhelming. Her brother smelled like this when injured severely as a young lion, also kicked in the head. He had slept for several days. Tuft watched her mother and waited until the skyline to the east shone morning red. Perhaps her mother was resting.

She remained standing as she waited. Her mother lay still. One of her eyes was closed. The other blankly stared as Tuft circled and looked into the eye. Unsure of her choices, she decided to leave her mother and go back for her brother. He might realize the gravity of the situation when he saw her.

Tuft doubted that would be true but had no other choices.

Red watched behind the Kinnikinnick shrubs, knowing he blended in well. His held-open eyes resembled the low-to-the-ground crimson berries. His father had taught him this.

For several hours, Red studied the prone animal he'd found, sure now it was dead. The smells were that of a deceased animal. The animal's hair pattern, the rise of the lying haunch, one eye strangely open, and an ear bent awkwardly down all confirmed the carcass was a lion. He had not walked up to it. With every giant beast comes awful surprises. Unknown dangers from animals who feast on foxes emerge without warning. The lion may just be pretending, like Red was doing in the bushes.

After careful and patient waiting, Red readied to approach. In the remaining darkness, he policed the area one more time. There! From below, a lion very much alive stepped up from the creek. Its head was down. Red's caution had paid off. If he'd stepped out a moment earlier the animal would have easily leapt at Red.

The lion was walking, though, not stalking. Red could tell it was a female. He knew the genitalia of lions. The female was to be especially feared. Walking meant this lion wasn't looking for food. Red guessed the dead animal must be familiar to her. She did not hesitate upon her approach.

He thought about running away. Too close. Too late. He remained still, low in the evergreen growth.

The lion stopped and nudged the head of the carcass, poking it with her paws and snout. Then, she simply stared. Red did not move. The female lion stayed quiet, studying the dead animal. She then circled it. She looked back down the way she had come many times, but not with any regularity. Red couldn't time her turned head away to make his getaway.

A fox can be motionless for a long time. Red knew that. But each minute that went by was more nerve-racking than the last. Lions know the smell of fox better than any other animal. He assessed his options and hoped that the sour, sharp smell of the dead lion, the very aroma that had attracted him to it some time ago, would overpower his scent.

Best to stay still and take his chances. Lions were much faster than he. This lion already had the advantage. He would have to turn and run if she sensed him. He held a ready stance, flat to the ground, crouching, and calmed his heart.

Tuft's head pounded, maybe from lack of food, she thought, maybe from the shock of her mother's state. No saliva in her mouth meant she needed water, too.

She finally turned away from her unmoving mother and walked back to the creek. The image of her lifeless mother did not match anything she remembered.

As Tuft reached for a drink in the creek, she heard the sound of distant barking. The husky noise was too low of a pitch for coyotes. She couldn't determine how near they were. Maybe wolves. But, in the morning? That's not right.

She crept into an open area where the creek rounded into the canyon floor before disappearing into the higher brush but saw nothing. Tuft spied a stand of pines opposite from the direction of her family's den. The trees stood below this part of the creek. She quickly ran to them for cover.

She thought then of her brother. He didn't hear sounds well and might not pick up the noise. He could smell better than she, though. He should pick up the scent of the wolves, right? She couldn't smell any wolves — just a soapy whiff of unknown sweat and hair.

Instead of heading back to the ridge where she'd left her brother, Tuft scampered down into the canyon to lead the barking animals away, just in case, and then she would double back. As she slipped through low-hanging tree branches, she looked for the wolves. The sound had moved. They were either headed up the canyon or crossing the canyon to one side. Which side she had no idea.

Had they picked up the smell of her mother? The thought shook her. What could they do to her now? She put the notion away, afraid for her life in a new, more frightening manner but not eager to dwell upon it.

Tuft already traveled too far down into the canyon. She was unfamiliar with this area and decided to cross the canyon floor, dash between rocks and brush to the other side. That's where she would then head back up to the den and be sure her brother was aware of the intruders. Together, they could fend off any group of animals.

The scare of the wolves surged energy into her body, yet that power quickly slipped into fear. All she could conjure were negative possibilities from the worry that pushed her to get back to her brother, plus her likely dead mother. She had never been courageous or optimistic, and now she was alone and afraid too.

Along the way back, she smelled their old den, where they had until recently lived. It lay hidden on the same side of the canyon where she was traveling. She was surprised by the remaining scent of lion. Her family hadn't been in that den for some time.

She listened but couldn't hear the noise of the wolves. Perhaps they had headed up the other side after all.

The smell came back again, stronger this time. Tuft looked up into the dark of the rock, a well-suited, almost invisible entrance. Had her brother come back here?

After the bothersome lion finally left the dead carcass behind, Red decided to act before another animal came by. He'd been considering how to cover up the found food for some time, properly saving the meat. The dead lion would last a long time. The plan had to go into effect right now. Yes, he thought. Now.

Red leaped from his hiding place and set to digging a hole for the animal. The pit needed to be next to it. He started at the top, near its head, and formed a dugout for a long and wide trench the entire length of the lion. He began at the head and worked his way down. As he dug deeper, he had to be careful that the body wouldn't fall on him. He was bigger than most foxes, he knew, but caution was the order of the day.

He dug like he was creating a new home, urgent, furious, and with all his might.

Tuft studied the area around her family's old den, hidden well among rocks and behind oak brush halfway up the canyon wall. Their mother had moved them onto a ridge, not closer to water but no longer in the cave. Tuft wasn't sure why. She figured since she no longer brought water to them, that must have been the reason. That's when she and her brother had learned to drink out of the creek.

Tuft crept up to the den to check it — just to take a glimpse. Besides, she was tired. Maybe she could rest. Her brother might be there, snoozing away.

When she looked in, expecting her old empty home or maybe her brother, she saw a female lion with two kittens looking directly at her.

Neither lion reacted immediately. The presence of the other startled each into the ancient, practiced gaze of cats in opposition. Tuft did not know where that instinct came from or even that she had such a skill.

A strange memory filled her mind as she took in the scene. A longing, ogling image of a mother with two kittens, sitting in the exact position of her mother, in a place where she once lived. She had missed that time here, and she remembered the comfort of this place.

This mother glared at her with wider eyes. She had an older face, framing a power Tuft did not have. Tuft returned a similar glare, though purely instinctual, with her paws tight beneath her snout. On the uphill graveled entrance to the den, she was prone, looking at a picture of her earlier life, absorbing the scene in front of her, squinching her face to match that of the mother lion.

Tuft's body went slack a bit, losing her concentration. She thought about her mother, dead by the creek.

The female in the cave cupped her kittens behind her left front leg, shielding them and bracing herself for a fight. The mother was afraid of her, Tuft realized. She looked more protective than scared, though. Tuft felt her bowels release, but she had not eaten, so nothing happened. A slight shaking of Tuft's eyebrows expressed the only movement on her face.

The mother lion lifted her head, a sign of aggression that Tuft recognized. She watched the lioness protecting her kittens with the gradual spread of all four of her paws. She was shifting to attack position.

Tuft had never been in confrontation with a lion other than her mother and brother. The genuine danger of this encounter mounted with each movement of the mother lion, readying to jump. Tuft finally grasped the point of the growing ferocity from the lion who wanted her to leave. Tuft was not a kitten anymore. This lion saw a full-grown predator, not a pining kitten.

No, Tuft thought. I'm not here for that.

Tuft rapidly pushed her body backward, down the dirt path entrance to the den, dropping beneath the opening. She slid over the gravel, falling to the path, then stood up and turned away from her old home. Tuft did this slowly, turning her back to the mother lion to show submission. She knew about submission.

After a few steps, Tuft bolted. She ran up the side of the canyon, racing back to her brother. Tuft shook her head as she ran. Time to focus. She needed to get back to her brother and show him where their mother lay and somehow point out the presence of another lion in their old home. Oh, and there were the wolves, too.

Now, more urgent than before, she also had to get something to eat. She knew with learned shame that she was not much of a hunter. She had watched but never had to kill or even capture food. Her mother had focused on her brother for that. He learned quickly. Soon, she had to fight him off. He liked to practice on her, hitting, bumping, and grabbing her with his teeth.

Tuft knew her mother had to spend more time with him to assure the sharing of food with his sister. But now, they no longer had their mother. Tuft had to think differently about kills and meals.

As her brother grew larger than her mother, so had Tuft developed. She saw the look in that mother's eyes. Tuft was fully grown but not very grown-up. How would she ever learn to be a lion?

In a short time, she was back at the carcass of the deer kill from last night, breathing hard. Her brother was not there and, unsurprisingly, did not bother to bury it. Their mother always cleaned up.

The red hue at the horizon quickly turned to bright sunlight. Tuft confirmed that nothing remained on the carcass. It was smaller than she thought. Then she saw a part was missing. Her brother must have hidden it. She poked around but found nothing.

Already ants were crawling over everything. Tuft had seen bears do it, so she licked at the ants. They moved too much and crept all over her face. Eating ants was not a good solution.

Tuft had not slept for some time and now was thirsty again. She drank very little at the creek. The ants in her mouth and on her face didn't help. Seeing her mother by the stream had ruined her focus. Her mother would not be getting her food. She squinted at her new circumstance and cried quietly as if her brother could hear her. He couldn't, though. She shook with panic.

Think, she told herself. She might crack open the carcass for some nourishment in the bones, she thought. Yes, but later. First, she would find her brother and take him to their mother. Then, water. Maybe he would grasp that it was now his responsibility to feed her.

Maybe she should cover the carcass with dirt as her mother did.

No, find her brother first.

He must share with her.

He had to take care of her now.

That prospect did not comfort her.

Red gnawed off what he would take with him. After bumping his side at the lion and rolling it into the pit he'd dug, he ate what he could. If another animal found his cache, he wanted to prepare a different storage place for some of it. He covered the rest of the lion, packing down the ground with his paws. He scrambled about the area, attempting to hide his digging. The attempt, however, was not very successful.

The lion was bigger than any other cache he had dug. Much larger. At best, he could mask the smell with the dirt. The dirt barely covered the body up. It would have to do.

Grabbing his food, a sizeable carry of meat, Red jogged away.

Tuft climbed to the rocks above the den, thinking her brother would be catching the morning sun. He was there, sleeping. He did not hear the wolves. She needed to rouse him, but Tuft was cautious. He did not awaken calmly. She needed to show him her mother's body, and also the occupied lion's den. They would need to move since another lion lived in the canyon for them to contend with.

She wondered if her mother knew about the other lion. No, she decided. Probably not. No matter. She was dead. Enough of the thinking, she told herself, shaking her foggy head. She was starving. Back to her brother.

She approached to nudge him awake. As she got closer, her brother's head abruptly jerked up off his paws and then quickly fell back where it was. His eyes didn't open. Tuft arched her back. She had never seen him do that before.

Blood came out the side of his head. She squeaked a high-pitched scream at him, the only noise she knew how to make that he could hear. But he didn't move. He hated it when she squealed. That, he should hear. No movement, though. She approached him and poked his body with her paw. Blood spilled out of his mouth.

How is this happening?

His body now looked suddenly like her mother's, lifeless. She could tell he was no longer breathing. Tuft was horrified. She watched her brother's body slackening, shrinking into the rocks. What had happened, she thought? She squealed at him.

Tuft heard barking again. Searching the ground below her, she saw some strangely colored animals out in the middle of the canyon, standing, looking up at her. The wolves she heard were near them. She stared back at them, squealed at them, and then the wolves took off to her left. They were coming after her, heading for the access to the rocks where she stood. She squealed at her brother again. It was no use. He, too, was dead. She turned, ran away from them, trying to focus on what she would do. Her brother was dead. Her mother was dead.

She didn't stop, moving as fast as she could through wooded areas down the canyon, on the northern ridge. She decided to go back down into the gorge below and cross to the other side.

RANDY

Oscar snapped at the dogs bouncing around him. He was the oldest, and the young dogs were making too much noise. Their excitement, however, was contagious. He got his howling in, too, but danged if they weren't unruly.

He looked at his human owner. Oscar didn't know he was owned, though. He considered the situation the other way around. The human brought him food, cleaned up his poop, brushed him, and drove him around in his truck. Heck, he did everything that Oscar wanted.

His owner rubbed the back of his ears, and Oscar knew he'd done an excellent job. He had led this band of pups on a terrific run. In the widespread limbs, high in the largest tree in the valley, hung a lion to prove it.

It was not the first lion he had treed. He and his owner had grown up together doing this. He stared up at the lion as the younger dogs clawed at the tree. He studied the lion's markings, something he liked to do. After a few minutes, Oscar strolled back to his owner and sat next to him.

Then, just as Oscar decided his owner should give him a treat, there it was.

Perfect.

Two of three hounds had chased a snarling mountain lion into a huge Edelman pine tree. They bounced around the tree's trunk, scratching up the bark and kicking dust everywhere in the ordinarily quiet area at the bottom slope below the south-facing ridgeline. The sun had been up only a little while.

Three orange-jacketed hunters had taken positions around the tree, though only one of them had a hunting license. He was also the only one who had a rifle. The other two were just watching. The dogs had done all the work and kept the lion trapped in a crook of two large branches.

One of the men had his hands in his pockets. He was taking everything in after running farther than he had in years, chasing the dogs with a lion on the run. His name was Steve. They had rather quickly found the lion, he thought, and the hunt went just as Randy had outlined.

"Be best to shoot it in its habitat," Randy said earlier. "But chasing it into a tree is the next best thing."

About an hour ago, when they arrived at the base of the canyon, the dogs took off quickly, racing uphill. They smelled a lion, all right. Probably more than one. Steve hadn't seen the animal clearly until now, except afar when they saw it up on the rock ledge. He didn't know that lions squealed like that. There it was, now, though. He assumed this was the same lion. Fifteen feet up in a tree, as close to a lion he'd ever been. It screeched again, an awful noise that hurt everyone's ears. Lions squealed? It must be the same one that cried out earlier, right before Randy fired his rifle.

Randy, the one with the license, checked the butt of the lion and reported that the lion was a female. He didn't call them lions, though. He called them cougars.

"Now we can see. Couldn't tell the cougar's gender back there high in the rocks. We can now, though. The dogs did good," Randy said dryly amid the din of barking. "But we're not bagging this one." Randy dropped his rifle into the crook of his arm.

He rubbed his dog's ears. Oscar, a Bluetick Coonhound, was his. The rest of the canines, two different mixed-breed hounds, were from a rescue breeder's compound. Randy finally got the chance to take them out.

The young man, not yet twenty years, had earlier fired a warning shot at the rocks beneath the lion when they'd spied her up at the top of the ledged stones. The dogs had headed the hunting party up farther into the canyon when they spied her. The entire canyon seemed full of lion scents.

Hunts usually started slowly, but the dogs wanted to dash off as soon as they hit the canyon. The dogs were kept quiet on the first part of their hike up the canyon, following Oscar's lead, just like Randy had trained him. They went to the right, north, about halfway up the canyon, and then they shifted back to the middle, heading pretty much west. The scent had the dogs agitated. Randy could tell when dogs were on the lion's scent. Oscar was the first to notice.

They began barking too soon. Randy tried to hush them, but they wanted to take off. Fortunately, he had them on their leashes. But that only made them bark more.

Neither Randy nor his friends saw any lions until they reached the top of the canyon. Just as they were going farther west, they heard a strange cry, almost like a coyote. The dogs quieted when they heard that.

Looking up to their right, on a rocky ridge, Randy and the others saw the lion. She was making a strange coyote-like noise at the rocks beside her. None of them knew it was a female at that point. That's when he took aim and fired off a shot at the rock near where she was making that noise to see if she would turn away, and they could see her rump.

She wasn't spooked much, just a slight jump. Then, she smelled the spot where he had fired and hit the rock. She squeaked that noise some more, several times in fact, and the dogs couldn't hold off. They started barking at her.

Looking back at them, she bolted away. That's when Randy let the dogs go on the chase. He had explained at length to his two uninitiated friends that this added April hunt — a rare, special season — did not usually allow for the harvesting of any female lions. They'd teased him about missing the shot, and he explained why he fired without hitting the lion.

He'd wanted the lion to turn and look up behind her, not down at them, and then they could see the tail. A bump of skin over the rump, covering the anus, meant she would be a female. A visible anus revealed it as male.

She didn't do that, though. The noisy dogs ruined the ruse. The dogs chased her down the canyon to the tree where they now stood — quite a run.

At the tree, Randy had to explain again that he could only harvest a male.

"Harvesting?" Anthony, the third man, yelled, more than asked. "You guys are killing the danged animals. Why the euphemism? Just say what it is, for goodness's sake!"

Anthony was not going to be invited on a hunt again, Randy decided. His anti-hunting friend had no idea about the point of hunting. Several times he made accusing remarks like that. He should have questioned Anthony earlier and saved himself this grief. Why did he even come? His other charge, Steve, seemed engaged in the rare opportunity.

Licenses limit the number and gender of each take, and Randy had a male license. "It is harvesting," Randy muttered. Too many of the cats left to populate, he explained, and they would eliminate every species in a matter of a few short years. Then the cougars would starve and head into the urban areas.

"They'd end up getting destroyed later, but in anger," he said a little louder. He wanted to explain that lions get killed for attacking pets.

Frightened homeowners don't help the plight of lions. It's best to harvest up high in the forest a fixed number of lions so they don't head into neighborhoods.

"Angry kills," Randy called them. Those are not healthy for anyone.

Anthony paid close attention to Randy's explanation.

"We're just trying to keep a balance," Randy said.

Anthony shrugged, a bit defiant, but he recognized Randy's logic. The concept made sense. The sight of the frightened lion bothered him. Still, they were going to let this one go. That accounted for something.

The two dogs with Oscar had earlier identified some very young lion kittens, only days old, hiding in some bushes about 50 yards away from this tree, and wouldn't let up their barking. The brush was too condensed, but they could see the kittens. Randy investigated and discovered them cleverly hidden in the bush. He had to tie the two younger dogs to a tree several yards away to keep them from bothering what he now suspected were offspring of the mother they had driven into the tree above them.

He had spied the lion first thing in the morning, but she took off up the canyon. Must have heard the dogs and then hid her kittens. Randy wondered how to let the mother down safely but figured she'd run for her kittens once they let her go.

"You must be pretty upset, eh?" Anthony teased Randy. "Nothing to kill. Or, harvest, as you say."

Randy took off his sunglasses and rubbed his eyes with the back of one of his hands, shaking his head. But when he looked over at Anthony, the young man just smirked. Randy wanted to say that the chase, the discovery, and the opportunity were really what all this was about. He didn't have the energy. Instead, he smiled back.

"Guess not," Anthony said, shrugging. "Kind of fun, though, getting to see the cougar up close. That why you're smiling?"

Randy blinked hard, surprised. He nodded in favor of Anthony's assessment. Might have misjudged the fellow. Hope for him, yet.

Tuft shivered from fear, her legs hanging every which way over the two branches she'd managed to climb after running from the agitated wolves. There were too many for her to fight off. She had been running from one danger to the next since she had stepped out from behind a hill of boulders earlier that day.

She tried to relax on the branches, breathing hard while she kept the three funny-looking, long-eared wolves in her view. Her head was almost spinning as she kept inventory on the odd-acting animals. They jumped at her from the ground below.

The large standing creatures around the tree looked odder than the wolves — bright skin the color of some bird feathers, constantly upright on two legs. The wolves seemed to ignore the tall animals like they weren't there. The tallish creatures looked up at Tuft and growled. Well, they were purring maybe, in a strange array of sounds. Periodically, their arms would jut out at each other. Their heads, though, held huge, dark eye sockets. These creatures were very strange to Tuft. She saw one of the creatures remove their eyes and rub tiny holes behind them with the back of their arm's paw.

The wolves, though, were what she had to think about right now. What was she going to do? Just stay up here until they left, she supposed. She tried to catch her breath and get ready if she had to fight one or even all of them.

She wondered where the mother lion and her kittens had gone. She had run by her on the ridge's edge, covering her escape from these strange intruders to the canyon. But she didn't see the kittens with her. Tuft was confused about everything, flustered, and now trapped.

She was still hungry, exhausted beyond memory, and feeling any reserves of energy shake out of her. Maybe she could jump down and surprise them, then grab one of the wolves and outrun them. Would that work? Time could be running out.

She'd deal with the tall creatures later if she could survive those strange-looking wolves.

The kittens were still relatively small, tucked into leaves so tightly that no one would see them. Their mother had taught them this. They huddled together, purring bodies humming in unison. They squeezed harder on their closed eyes, pretending they were in their home where it was dark, where the ground was warm, and where they could smell their mother.

SNARL WATCHES

Crouched on a stony ledge and looking down into the wide-bottomed lowland canyon, Snarl took in the new ravine he'd just entered. He had already crossed through three previous gorges with similar widening valleys that dropped into the plains below. He listened at each canyon area for prompts that urged him to mark out his territory. At the last valley he'd run into a bear. He continued his trek.

Snarl felt no urgency, only a sense to push on. At this valley, for the first time, he smelled lion. The scent floated down, coming from the top of the canyon to his left. The smell of lions might frighten most young cats away. The opposite happened to Snarl. The place felt and smelt like home.

Barking noises filled the valley. Not coyotes, and not wolves. Different. Snarl crept along the sunny side ridge of the canyon to hide his scent, stopping about halfway to the sunrise end of a gigantic crack in the mountain that had made the canyon. He began to identify lots of activities. This was a busy place, alive with animals. He made himself as invisible as he could. Then he took in the information.

A lion was running up the canyon, a female, almost like it was coming at him. Before getting too close, she veered toward his side of the ridge but not up to the top. She hung against the ridge wall below him. The sun had barely popped over the horizon. The lion, likely a mother, looked behind her periodically, stopping more than heading up.

Farther down, Snarl spotted some weird coyotes. No, they were more like wolves. Bigger than coyotes, but their front and rear haunches matched in size. These animals were new to him. Their heads swiveled too much, and they bounded over each other like they were playing. Each one struggled like something was pulling their necks. Their ears fell to the sides of their heads like large tongues.

Below the coyote-like wolves, Snarl saw strangely colored, skinny bears. They stood upright and surrounded the tree where the wolfy things pranced around. Probably something in that tree they want, Snarl considered. It was quite a distance, but Snarl had practiced looking farther and farther away throughout his early years. He saw nothing where the wolves were focused.

The approaching lion below him was getting too close. He scootched away from the ledge so the wind on the ridge would blow his smell away, south. She walked like his mother. A female, then. He thought of backing up all the way but remained perched and still. She was looking back more and more as she got closer and finally came to a halt about 50 yards away. Snarl didn't sense that she knew he was there. He was now above and behind a stand of rocks, hindering his visibility even further. She turned her back to him, watching below like he had been doing. Snarl cocked his head, trying to figure out what the other lion was thinking, what she was watching. Perhaps, she too, was wondering about the strange wolves and the skinny colorful bears.

Snarl decided to stay up, hidden on the ridge, and move farther along the right ledge of the canyon to get a closer look at the tree where the bears were standing. He was careful to stay out of the sight-line and earshot of the lion below. This may be her territory, and he did not want a confrontation. Not yet.

He slowed his steps to match the drift of the clouds, which would be in her line of sight above the ridge. Snarl moved slowly because the female lion was pacing back and forth now, still staring down at the commotion around the tree. Her vigilant eyes might pick up any pattern shifts in the brush where he hid. Her concentration, though, remained fixed on the animals below her. She did not appear concerned with the ridge above. Snarl moved slowly down through the oak scrub.

If she turned and continued her escape from the wolves up to this steepest part of the canyon, he couldn't continue forward without being in her peripheral vision.

Snarl stopped as he heard short, sharp tweets, like birdcalls, maybe coming from the bears. The wolves ran toward the bears. One of the bears had gathered the other two. One wolf stood still at one of the bear's legs. Snarl had never seen such a strange sight. Even with all the howling, the wolves' tails wagged happily. They were playful, which didn't fit the scene for Snarl.

The female lion stopped her pacing as the bears stayed on their hind legs and then walked down the canyon, away from Snarl and the female lion. The coyote-like wolves followed, barking and continuing to jump over each other.

Snarl was happy to see them go.

The female then began creeping back down the canyon floor, heading in the direction of the bears and wolves, her head low to the ground. Snarl copied her speed, remaining above her line of vision along the ridge. She may also be curious about the tree. Or, he thought, she was stalking the pack of bears and wolves.

Wolves and bears, though, are not usually stalked by lions. Crawling, hidden in a roll of oak brush, Snarl matched her progress.

Then, Snarl noticed a herd of deer walking ahead of him, coming from his right, across the flat top of the ridge. He stopped. He hadn't eaten in a few days. They weren't quite close enough for a chase, he calculated. Food suddenly jumped ahead of his curiosity about the canyon below. He needed to eat.

The deer hadn't noticed him because he was well camouflaged. Fortunately, the wind was blowing upwind of the deer. They probably didn't pick up his scent. If they had, they'd be off racing.

Following the path down the edge of the ridge in front of him, the deer headed into the canyon. Their direction aimed the herd toward the same tree, watched by both he and the female lion. Snarl lost eyeshot of the lion below him. He was crouched too low to the ground.

Snarl wondered when she would spot the deer and what she would do. One of the young fawns wandered beyond the others, nibbling into the brush. Snarl's hunger kicked in at the sight of the fawn.

He could see the doe and the other fawns continuing along the trail, led by a large buck. Snarl marked off the distance. A few more yards, and it would be easy for him to take down the fawn and be off.

The female lion was still out of sight but must be in a similar position as he, though farther below. The herd was headed her way and moving away from him. Snarl considered that she wouldn't attack with the large buck in front but wait for the deer to pass. That's what he would do.

Snarl would not have the chance once she leaped at the herd. They might run back up the ridge, back to him, or head the other way, toward the bottom of the canyon. He couldn't assess for sure. This lagging fawn would make up his mind, he decided. If it gets any closer, he'll take it. If not, he'll await his chances when the female scatters them.

The mother lion, named Claw by her mother, stood watching from a safe spot up the canyon. She wished the dogs hadn't spooked her. She might have waited them out in the den, but Claw wasn't one for waiting when it came to dogs, foxes, coyotes, or wolves. She could fight off a couple of them, but that den smelled strongly of lion. They could easily track where she and the kittens hid. It was better to get the kittens into the brush and then lure the dogs into chasing her up the canyon.

She already knew about these kinds of dogs. Men took them out to hunt with them. But Claw had miscalculated their interest. The dogs must have gotten onto the kittens before chasing after her.

She put Scratch and Scruff into the thickest brush she could find, up high. Then she took off directly for the dogs. Claw was sure they'd see her and follow her. She flew right below the last one in the pack. He barked at her immediately, and she took off up the mountain toward the beginnings of the ravine. At first, Claw looked like she would go to the bottom of the ridgeline, but then she turned and started bounding up the canyon, into the open, to keep their attention on her.

The dogs turned away from her, suddenly. They heard birds or something making tweet noises. How could they have not followed her? She was so obvious. Claw took several bounding leaps to get their attention, but they went the opposite way, directly for her kittens.

Her heart sank. She heard nothing but barking, constant barking. Claw continued up the canyon, hoping they would spy her there and come after a larger prize.

But then, maybe she was wrong? That other female lion had been by her den earlier that morning. Maybe they found her. Or, perhaps the other lion found the kittens. Was that the tweeting? Is that what kittens sound like when being attacked? Claw didn't know. Her kittens had never been attacked or bothered by anything.

Claw had too much to process. Too many things could be possible. She paced back and forth in the open on the ridge, but none of the dogs had taken chase. Their barking wouldn't allow her to return. Not yet.

She continued her back and forth motions while looking for a sign of the dogs or the other female lion. If they came her way, she'd circle the ridge and look for her kittens. She might have to fight off the other lion. Would that other female steal them? Stealing kittens was not a lioness desire that she could recall.

Claw thought back about how she found an orphaned kitten not long ago. It was in a brush area, much like the one where she left her little ones. She waited a whole night, but no lion came. By the time she had gotten to the kitten, it was dead. It had probably been there for a very long time.

Scratch and Scruff will not have to wait long, she assured herself as she paced. If they are alive, she'll have them back in no time. She didn't consider what she would do if the dogs had found them. She hoped the other lion would find them first. That lion would do the same as she had and wait one night. Right?

The barking faded. Not that it went away, but it was moving out.

One night's wait won't be necessary.

Sharp Eyes took his herd as far from the valley as he could. He figured the move would take them away from the lion and the rambunctious bear back on the creek two ravines behind them. In any case, it was time to move. The cold season had been over for some time. The fawns had been born, and the ground was dry.

He didn't push them, allowing everyone to graze as they went. He watched for movement, sniffed for smells in the wind, and listened for noises. He stretched a typical day's rounds into the warming season's migration.

Barking had pushed their travel up into the higher climb of an upcoming ridge. He heard a familiar animal bark and circled his herd into wide rings as they moved from the lower elevations to span outwards and deeper away from the extended spring valley they just left. Round and round they went, making good progress, even as they appeared to predators to be heading in no real direction.

They would not go back to the valley with the spring creek until the warm season began cooling.

The barking noises moved lower and away. Sharp Eyes could hear the noises as the wind blew up and over the canyon. He took the herd, slowly, to the ridge, following a trail he'd crossed several times over his lifetime. Sharp Eyes tasted the grass tips, resolved that more moisture lay ahead. Leaving the spring valley and ready water meant he would need to find a new stream soon. He had to keep the does and their fawn assured that he knew what he was doing. The grass was good news.

Sharp Eyes looked back at Prance. She always stayed at the back end of the herd. He wondered if she did that to exit for another, younger, stronger buck or if she just liked following up. Her attention to detail allowed Sharp Eyes to concentrate more on the way ahead. Prance's fawn would be just like her, he thought, as the little one looked in the same directions as her mother. The other fawns strayed farther from their mothers, eating and playing.

He enjoyed watching them bounce and run in fits and starts. Their youth reminded him of the freedom he had known as a young buck. Prance's fawn paid no attention to the other fawns. The young deer mimicked her mother in everything.

The other fawns were carefree and a marvel in their budding graceful movements.

Those are the ones we'll lose, he knew.

STARVING

Tuft watched the noisy crowd leave her.

The wolves barked the entire time, even after they were dragged away by the bears. Why did they go with them? No matter. Tuft hadn't noticed how labored her breathing had become until she could no longer hear the yapping noises. Her body shook from fear.

She more fell from the tree than jumped. Unprepared for this outcome, Tuft scrambled in several directions, wondering which way she should go. In addition to the fright of being chased and then treed, she was also thirsty. Tuft wasn't sure if her dizziness was due to the lack of water or her hunger. She took refuge beneath some bushes to calm herself down.

Before Tuft could fully decide which way to head, a stampede of deer came flying over the brush behind her. They landed on their hooves just feet in front of her. She was so surprised by the rush of leaping deer that she simply watched them bounce away.

Tuft felt hopeless about her situation. She had little idea about chasing deer down. She never initiated any hunt that she could remember. Her role consisted of corralling deer, which primarily meant that she got out of the way so her mother or brother could make a kill.

She remembered killing a ground squirrel when she was younger. She bit it after the pesky animal jumped on her nose. She'd also chased after a young elk, but she couldn't subdue it. She rode on its back until it hopped into some branches, and she fell off.

Tuft needed water. She'd wasted a lot of time wandering and circling. The sun had risen, and there wasn't any dew left to lick off the grass. She didn't want to go back up to the top of the canyon because of her mother and brother's lifeless bodies. She was afraid that she might die next. As a compromise, she decided to hike up to the other ridge of the canyon and see if she could find some additional stream there.

As she walked, Tuft felt foolish that she had never paid attention when she went on hunts with her mother and brother. She couldn't recall any of the territories where she was walking. She spent most of her time keeping clear of her brother, who would nip at her legs or come bounding out of nowhere and knock her down.

Her mother looked out for her but was primarily concerned about her brother. Tuft hung her head to the ground, sniffing like her mother did, wondering if she could pick up the scent of water. She was wandering, she knew, trekking in all kinds of directions as she climbed upwards to the ridge.

As Tuft came over the edge of the ridge, she felt the strain in her shoulders and back legs. She was weary beyond her memory. Other than the constant harassment of her brother, she couldn't remember feeling this confused, dizzy, and groggy.

Her head followed her nose as she walked. She crested the ridge and then haplessly meandered into a trench. She felt more comfortable hiding in the trench, she told herself. Just after she headed into it, she slipped and rolled all the way down.

Tuft picked up the smell of blood, deer blood, but couldn't trace its direction. As soon as she dropped into the long trench, the bloody scent went away. She stopped and realized the smell came from behind, and she turned around. Her nose still scuffling just above the dirt, she walked out of the trench and stopped. There, at the opening, stood a mountain lion, gripping a young fawn in his teeth. He held the deer easily. He was staring at her.

At first, Tuft thought it was her brother, and she slowly sat back on her rear haunches, eyes wide at what she saw. Blood dripped down the neck of the fawn. That's what she smelled, she thought.

The lion exuded confidence. It wasn't like Tuft's brother at all. This lion's eyebrows were thinner and his shoulders more prominent. A streak of his hair was a light color, like when lions are just puppies. He was not a puppy, though. His body didn't twitch, and his ears pointed straight up. She remained on her haunches, her body wavering from weakness. She blinked twice and fell to her right. She fainted from hunger and exhaustion.

Claw saw the wolves and bears head back down the canyon. She lowered her shoulders and rushed toward her kittens. This time, she moved into the brush and hid her movements.

After only a few yards, she couldn't hold back her worry, and she bolted through the trees on a tear back to the brush where she put Scratch and Scruff. She feared the worst. Disregarding the slap at her eyes of the thicker branches and the tears on her ankles from the bramble thorns, she arrived.

There they were. Snuggled together. Safe.

Claw stretched her body into the brush, turned her head and plucked one after the other, and put them at her feet. They were fine. The kittens moved their legs and arched their backs, waking up. Claw was surprised that they suffered no harm.

She canvased the area and listened for the return of the wolves. She picked up the smell of lion coming in two directions and a distant smell of lion up the canyon. She hadn't been paying attention. Her mind was on the boys.

The only way was up the side of the canyon in front of her. She gently rolled the kittens to grasp both of their backs in her mouth. She knew the trail behind the den that went up the canyon. That's where she would go.

She purred to the kittens.

They were getting out of this place.

Tuft tasted blood. It wasn't hers. She recognized the tinny flavor of deer blood. She licked, but her eyes were still closed. A renewed strength quickly surged through her body. She tasted deer meat in her mouth, and chewed.

After quite a while slowly eating and feeling the tingling in her jaw go away, Tuft finally opened her eyes. The haunch of a deer angled across her mouth. She gnawed the meat more aggressively and worked her body into position to look over the deer and see what had happened. She remembered seeing a lion and then nothing.

She had passed out many times in her life, but that was from her brother pressing against her neck. This time was different. She'd passed out from exhaustion and lack of water.

Tuft eyeballed the area in front of her, seeing that she was still in the trench area, though a little farther in than she remembered. She then turned to her left, and there was the same lion. She recognized his ears.

His back was to her. He was standing guard at the opening of the trench, or so it seemed. She was still chewing away at the deer haunch when the lion turned his head back to her. He looked for just a few seconds, and then he turned back again.

He is a different kind of lion, she thought.

Tuft ate the meat and began crunching on the bone to get to the marrow. She was feeling better as every minute went by.

The lion glanced her way a few times but didn't move from where he was. Tuft was still weak. If he turned to come at her at some point, she would back away. For now, she got her fill.

Tuft spied the rest of the fawn. He had buried it in the sidewall of the trench. She wondered if he had eaten about as much as she had. She couldn't tell, but he left no bones or scraps from his meal. This lion knew how to hunt and how to eat.

Tuft was surprised at how exhausted she was. She had gone too long without eating. She needed to rest, unsure if she could. Then the lion laid down on the ground, glancing back at her first. He faced outward, beyond the trench.

Good, Tuft thought. He must be resting now, too. She licked her face and front paws clean, then put her head down on her front legs. Soon, she was fast asleep.

Snarl watched the lioness he assumed he had been tracking earlier. She was very weak, having stumbled into the spot he'd found. She looked worn out, confused, and much younger than he expected.

He noticed extended teats for feeding young ones earlier, but up close this female looked haggard and bewildered. It must just be the sagging skin, he thought, still fixated upon his picture of the female lion he watched from the ridge.

Snarl had easily snatched the wandering fawn and turned back into this offshoot cut into the ridge, looking for a place to eat. The female lion rolled down the dirt into the trench. She fell with awkward movements, legs, and body uncontrolled.

When the lion finally noticed him, she had begun walking out of the trench. Amazed, Snarl watched as she walked toward him, with her head down. Her head lifted with a start when she finally saw him, and then she sat back on her rump. Her behavior looked familiar to Snarl, similar to his last trek with Spit. Except this lion was in a much weaker state. He wondered what she would do. She fell over, passed out from fright or exhausted. He couldn't tell.

Snarl continued waiting and watching, but she didn't get up. She was unconscious. Slowly, with the fawn still gripped in his mouth, he walked toward her. He saw that she was barely breathing. She was too skinny, unwell.

He dropped the fawn and looked around the area to see if any other animals were around. The sound of the baying wolves had long gone. Snarl studied the young lioness. She was not the lion he had seen. This one had been running hard for a very long time.

Snarl decided to move her to safety. The trench behind her would be as good a place as any. He nudged her front paws, but she did not flinch. He walked behind her. Snarl rumpled the skin of her neck into his mouth, then dragged her to a safer place, deeper in the trench.

He was surprised at how light she was. Scratches covered her body beneath several patches of torn hair. She must be either very young or highly malnourished. He had never seen a lion in this state before.

After he positioned her deep into the trench, he returned to the fawn, again scanning the area, and then brought the kill back toward her.

He was hungry. Judging by the female's appearance, she was too. He split the haunches of the deer into two, and noticing a dugout section in the trench wall, he dragged the rest of the kill into that section and kicked dirt and rock over it to hide it and conceal the smell.

He then dragged half of the deer's backside to the lioness, putting it near her snout, and he sat down and devoured his portion of the kill.

After finishing, he could see twitching in the legs of the lioness. He couldn't drag her near water, so he lifted the deer meat and let the blood drain into her mouth. Quickly, her mouth began to move. She might awaken and bite at him. So, he laid the haunch over her snout and backed away.

He then walked to the entrance of the trench and kept his eyes out for intruders. He glanced back and saw that she had begun eating. He stood for a while, continuing his watch of the area, pleased that she understood she was to eat.

He needed to rest and digest his fill. He lay down in a flop, dust airing as he did. Snarl kept looking out at the ridge beyond the trench, wondering if whatever had frightened her would be coming this way. He looked back and was again pleased with how comfortable she was with him there. She had fallen asleep.

Snarl looked at her for a bit and kept watch. He wondered what it would mean for him to be with a female. He had only known his mother. He didn't pick up any dark feelings. The meeting of this lion and sharing his kill seemed appropriate.

Time would tell.

The contrast of a life filled with death against a life promised with no end beggars belief. Creation's humans struggle with the proposition. Yet, life after death never enters the imagination of any other creature.

Not as an idea, that is.

Humans consider heaven because of their yearning for life, a place after the curse of a short existence peppered with harsh limits. God must reveal heaven's promise to the human in order for it to be true, because humans can only hope for it.

For those whom God has told about heaven, they are charged with telling everyone else. No one can be as convincing as God, so testifying that heaven is real only encourages others to believe. They must hear from God himself. All those who know about heaven know this to be true.

Animals have no notion of heaven. They enter heaven as they left earth — walking, flying, ambling, and crawling forward — driven by the Spirit that formed them and prompted from a place of authority that all creatures both fear and yearn for. Animals do not testify to each other, because they have no knowledge of God or heaven. Designed to live, however, even as they all succumb to an eventual, short, inevitable end, both human and animal enter the same place.

Many humans and most animals hear no Spirit whisper to them, only death's temptations. They live fixed to death's grip. Death strangles all of life's creatures through everything from domination to starvation. Daily, every living thing must eat to survive. One animal dies as a victim for another to live. To those gripped by death, they see no other path. Predators also become victims to death. The unknown heaven awaits them, and death's violent rule ends forever. There are no victims or predators in heaven.

Chapter Four

SPRING

And in that day I will make a covenant with them, with the beasts of the field, and with the fowls of the air, and with the creeping things of the earth: and I will destroy the bow, and the sword, and war out of the land: and I will make them sleep secure.

—HOSEA 2:18

EGG

Red lived in a dugout hole below a rock crevice, a morning's jog from the top of the canyon. His cache of the lion parts he brought back from his discovery a few days ago would last him for quite a while. He knew, pretty soon, that larger animals would probably find and finish off the lion Red stashed in a hole.

The diligent fox hustled back the very next day to his buried carcass. His incomplete attempt at covering it up had proved him out. Coyote had moved into the area. He knew them. They were a constantly hungry group of animals, skulking through the forest and the canyon daily, scrounging for things to eat. They made a dent on the meat, and Red didn't want to be there when they came back.

Foxes don't think in terms of good news and bad news. Like any low-level predator, Red operated from a position of shrewd caution, a crafty mix of low expectations and busy confidence. The lion meat was only his for a while, he knew, but getting to it first gave him courage. Nonetheless, fresh lion food meant the coyotes would be occupied and satisfied. Also, one less lion to worry about.

Back at his foxhole, Red was getting a well-needed rest. The meat he had salvaged meant he could lounge and ponder for another day or two.

The sun warmed the rock above his home. When he could feel the increased heat coming from the rock, he could leave the hole and lie on the rock as he did now. Sitting on a high slant amongst pines and aspen growing everywhere, the view from his rock piqued Red's imagination. Yes, foxes have a dream state. Though limited, foxes are capable of somewhat long memories. He enjoyed these moments of being warmed, rested, and thinking fearlessly about things.

Red watched the sun's rays tipple through the new leaves on the aspens, sparkling on his rock. Why couldn't every day be like this, he wondered? He blinked at his little part of the world. The sun reached halfway up the farthest pine in the distance, and sunlight through the forest reminded him of something. He stood up.

Red heard the man singing.

Time to go get his egg.

Tuft watched the falcon flying in circles above her head. She had only recently connected the falcon with her mealtime. When younger, watching birds circling in the air, Tuft would get dizzy. She could tell that her strength was back because the ground didn't spin when she looked down.

She hadn't been hungry for two days. That didn't happen very often. She ate what the lion brought her. Each time she fed, the falcon was flying overhead.

Tuft didn't assume she could take any meat from Snarl's buried deer, from fear that he might attack her and because she hadn't done anything to justify the privilege. It was not her desire to upset this lion. She enjoyed Snarl's willingness to share, though perplexed why he did so.

The food was now gone. Insects were crawling all over the carcass.

The falcon might prove to be a meal, Tuft thought, staring up at it. She would have to catch it soon because the falcon might not come back when no more meat was available. She wondered if she could leap high enough to snag the bird? What's he up there flying around and waiting for?

Snarl left last night and had not come back. Without more food, he must have moved on. Tuft was up most of the night but not out hunting. She stayed in the trench because Snarl didn't signal that she should follow him. Earlier, he had urged her to follow him to water, but not last night. She waited for him to come back so she could go to the stream again. Tuft didn't sleep, thinking she might miss Snarl.

Standing was wearing her out. She was still weak.

Tuft sat down and waited to see if the falcon would fly down and she could grab it. After a few minutes, it increased its flight circle higher and floated away.

She looked at the ground, trying to remember where she and Snarl had gone for water. Tuft strung together the markers on the path they had walked, the smells, and the sun's placement in the sky. She was dizzy because of her thirst. She decided to head to the stream on her own.

Walking Eagle McDermott bounced in the driver's seat, steering his pickup over the patchy part of the pass between Spring Valley Canyon and Ridge Canyon. He came by this area almost every morning, making his rounds.

"Rounds," he said, laughing.

As a ranger, years ago, that's how he described his daily monitoring of the national forest. He took the term seriously then, circling the forest by copying the ring-like tracks of deer. Deer go round and round as they progress through their daily walks, grazing as they go. Even their seasonal patterns of migrating follow a circular path. It's their way of confusing predators.

Walking Eagle walked his rounds during his foresting job. Younger then, he rode the pickup and walked only when necessary. On the Clayhall ranch, roads were mostly straight, from point A to point B, east and west. Few roads went north to south on the front range of the Rockies. Most of the land in the foothills were ravines. Homes and outbuildings were built in the valleys.

Tom Clayhall built his home reasonably close to where the forest rose up into the mountains, on the north end of the property. He liked to be near the animals that roamed on his land. He hired Walking Eagle to keep a daily watch on the wild residents. His sizeable acreage matched the environs where lions, bears, and coyotes could live. He didn't have typical ranch animals, hadn't tried to even grow crops, so a wolf or two could safely hunt on his vast portion of front-range property.

A neighbor used a 40-acre patch at the valley's eastern edge to cycle his cattle's grazing needs for tax purposes. The rest was raw.

McDermott talked out loud when he drove his rounds. He didn't take notes, so it was his way of remembering things.

"Elk will be coming through the property," he said while bouncing on the north road that edged Clayhall Ranch and a state forest stretch of grassland.

"Must be a blessing that I can keep such good company with myself," he explained to nobody.

The radio in the truck worked sporadically in the canyons. Walking Eagle tired of trying to tune in to music or talk shows in certain parts of his travels around Clayhall's ranch. His daughter had given him a speaker to plug into his phone. It fit on the front windshield dash. He liked the music from his old friends who sang at the Flying W Ranch over in Colorado Springs. They called themselves the Wranglers. His daughter somehow put the music on his phone.

He hadn't figured out how to play it. No matter what he did, no sound. The speaker was dusty, unused, and yet, his treasure. The little blue box was a reminder that his daughter loved him.

McDermott attempted to sing the songs from memory. He didn't have a bad voice, he believed. His favorites were a couple of songs from Church school when he was young — *What Wondrous Love is This*, and *Be Still My Soul*. They were favorites mostly because he knew all the words.

He stopped at the height of the pass, a beautiful spot. He reached into the jockey box, as he called the glove compartment. Wrapped in a paper towel was the egg he put there this morning. Almost every morning.

Walking Eagle sang in his deep gravelly voice, his voice rising at the end of each line. "What wondrous love is this, O my soul, O my soul! What wondrous love is this, O my soul! while millions join the theme, I will sing, I will sing, while millions join the theme, I will sing!"

Walking Eagle placed the egg on the same low branch of a craggy brush oak. He walked about 20 yards from his truck into the woods and gently balanced the egg between pieces of bark and dead branch joints. Two branches stuck out sideways, formed like a slingshot. He turned and went back to his truck, then leaned on the passenger side fender.

He pulled out a stick of spicy elk jerky from a batch he'd prepared over the winter and waited. The sun was beautiful that morning. Still dry, though. The spring rains won't come for a few more weeks.

McDermott had gone through several more verses into his song, finished his jerky, and was about to head out.

"My, my," he said when the fox popped out from behind a pine.

He waved at the fox. He lightly grabbed the egg in his teeth and trotted away.

THE DEN

Pikes Beak watched the lion staring up at him. He'd been flying with the wind, floating with his left eye trained on the ground. He wasn't interested in the lion, only in the animals that would come by scavenging after scraps the lion left behind.

Why won't the lion go away?

He didn't see any leftovers for animals to scavenge. Still, this waiting game was going nowhere. The falcon rose higher and looked for some other movement. Perhaps he would find that flock of ravens. Not the best eating, but it was better than hanging around here.

Why won't the lion go away?

Snarl canvased the entire canyon. He found the discarded remains of two recently dead lions, but he didn't find any live ones on the hunt. Something had happened to these two, both very different deaths. He hadn't yet considered that Tuft might be a lone survivor.

One lion was older, over by the creek. Snarl could smell that both fox and coyote had been there. The water would not be suitable to drink. His mother taught him not to drink water when dead animals were near. Not for a time, anyway. Besides, that area would not make for a place to set up a den, having to chase animals away all the time. Once wolves and coyotes, and even fox, find carrion, any dead thing, they'll make a habit of coming back.

Yet, he was thinking about staying around here. A good den area would help him decide. The place by the dead female lion was not favorable.

Not far from there, he'd found the skin of another lion. It smelled male. Young, like him, by the color of the fur. This dead lion had also been partly eaten by coyotes, but no fox had been there. Ravens sat up in the trees. The rest was probably theirs. He'd have to keep an eye out for the coyote, though he knew they weren't going to bother him. But they would steal his food if he had any. Another item to consider on staying in this canyon.

Maybe something fell on the lion. Large boulders piled everywhere. Nothing, though, looked newly fallen. Snarl concluded the death occurred toward the top of the ridge, pretty close to where the canyon disappeared into the upper forest. He could see that lions, probably these two, had been living near there. Falling rocks don't make for a safe place either.

Snarl continued to familiarize himself with the area, wandering, sniffing, cataloging every detail. Lions had been living here, but these two had died up at the top of the canyon. That's when he made the connection of Tuft to these animals.

He followed a trail down toward the valley. On the way, he located a den tucked well into the ridge wall facing the sun's path. Some other lion had lived there, very recently. It had the smell of kittens and a mother. He picked up no male scents.

He was now near that den, waiting to see if another lion would come by. He waited quite a while. And now the sun came up, rather late for a lion and her kittens to return to a den.

Snarl walked back up the trail and perched on an outcropping quite a ways up the sunny side ridge of the canyon. It had a view of the den but was hidden from sight by brush growing onto the rock. He could tell from this spot if a lion was coming from any direction.

More and more, he liked the layout of this ridge with its walled-in den. He was upwind from it, so any returning lion would probably be in clear view and not know he was there.

The den was just a short walk to a spring he had been using the past few days. He looked at the other side of the canyon wall, deeper down, up the ridge where the creek traveled. A thin stream dripped between the rocks. Tuft's lion family probably used the creek where the older lion had died. The dribbling creek was better for cover than the open creek.

He thought about the young female he'd been feeding. She was a very quiet lion. Not like his mother or brother, but they were his only frame of reference. Not much to go on.

Snarl wondered which den was her home, the outcropping spot or the hole in the wall. Or did she only arrive as he did? She seemed unfamiliar with her surroundings.

She had quite a few tears, scratches, and bruises. Some were older. Snarl wondered if the wolves he'd seen had done that to her, though only a couple of her cuts seemed to be fresh.

A hard life, he reckoned.

She had followed him to the spring each day, walking back and forth, up and down the trail as they went. He'd had some trouble getting her to follow him. She was not like Spit, bounding all over. She retraced the route as they walked. Snarl found that curious.

At first, he thought she kept reconsidering that she should follow him but soon realized she was simply checking on the direction. Constantly. It was like she wasn't sure where they had come from, and she was studying the way back. He remembered doing that as a kitten. She was not a kitten, though.

Snarl noticed the sun had moved up into the sky. He was tired from the night. No lion was coming back to the den this late, so he could nap. Tuft may be waiting for him, though.

Then, he spied Tuft walking across the canyon floor where he considered heading back. She wasn't retracing her way but stopped every few steps.

Well, well, he thought. Tuft is headed to the den! Still, though, it seemed strange that she was so cautious. If this is her den, why is she so fearful?

Snarl studied her. Tuft was a very careful lion. He traced back where she had entered the canyon. She must have come down from the spring. He'd already drunk from it much earlier. He put his head down and watched her movements.

It took Tuft some time, but she reached the den's opening. She looked around several times before going in.

Snarl considered what he would do now.

Walking Eagle drove to the north end of the property. He had no fences to follow on any side of the ranch. The bulk of Clayhall's real estate was chiefly composed of hardscrabble land. Two sides bordered national forest — the west and the north. Little yellow signs about a hundred yards apart identified where the national forest began, but you might not see them if you came from the national forest. They faced the other way.

Forest hikers, hunters, and tourists used the road, too. They'd often wander onto Clayhall's land. That was the trade-off. If you don't fence, folks don't know.

Clayhall didn't have animals, though. He just had the land and had no desire to barricade the populations. Both Clayhall and McDermott agreed that the wild animals didn't understand property lines. Since he had no domestic or ranch animals to protect, Clayhall could keep his land open.

A forest road followed the property line. Kind of. It was really an emergency cut put in by the national forest fire crews a couple of years back. A fire had rapidly pushed through an area called Waldo Canyon. Even though it was miles south, roads on the far reaches, anything near national forest, were re-cleared or created in preparation for a rush of fiery disasters.

More than ten years earlier, the Hayman fire had cut a swath from south to north and put the fear of God into the forest folks. Both the north and south ends of the Clayhall ranch were ringed by other old roads, which the forest service also re-graded for fire lines, just in case they were needed.

The roads made for convenient pickup travel for McDermott. He had several favorite places where he'd park along the way of his straights, and then he'd hike around. After turning on the west road, he had now gone about a half mile east on the north road.

A herd of elk was walking across the road, heading north and west, along their regular migratory path. Walking Eagle had to stop. Elk don't give vehicles the right of way.

They were a majestic sight. Walking Eagle treasured watching them. They'd head into higher country, where the females would drop their young. As a ranger, he could monitor them in the parks. Not now. He'd only walk the forest when he was hunting or off work. The elk would be gone from the ranch for the summer, so he pulled over to stare at them like any other rubber-necked citizen.

After a few minutes of watching the elk, since he was already stopped, he decided to hike along a deer trail he hadn't been on for some time. He took his rifle with him. There may be predators following the elk, and he wanted to be prepared if they changed their minds and went after an old Indian instead.

He brought no jerky on this hike. No sense in smelling like he was good to eat. That notion made him laugh again.

Ravens were flapping their wings rather than floating around or jumping from tree to tree. Pikes Beak knew something was up. He didn't much care what they were excited about. Their behavior simply meant he'd need a different strategy to snag one.

He flew through the trees instead of dropping from above. This would be slower, but the falcon could focus easier on one or two of the ravens, maybe. From above, the raven's flapping created too much of a distraction for him, more challenging to predict where a raven would be when he got closer. He could shoot into the ravens from a lower angle and have a better chance.

Just as he was about to fly into the group of crazy acting birds, Pikes Beak saw what was causing the commotion. Coyotes. The ravens and coyotes were fighting over a kill. He could see one raven in the mouth of a coyote. That was surprising. Coyotes are usually scared away by these large birds. In any case, the area was too dangerous for a falcon. The coyotes were jumping all over the place, and if the falcon missed, ravens could ruffle him up.

Unhappy over the chaos, Pikes Beak lifted over the top of a tree to get out of the area. Disappointed but clear of teeth and claws, he climbed higher. He saw a man coming out of the valley from his new height. The man was headed into the forest. Pikes Beak knew him. This fellow had thrown Pikes Beak food into the air for him to catch.

The falcon buzzed him, swooping by several times, but got no reaction. No food! The man ignored him, jogging faster in the direction of the coyotes and ravens.

This day was not going as he had planned. Pikes Beak screeched at the man to let him know he was not pleased and took off after a herd of elk up ahead. Maybe they smashed some animal on their trek, he hoped, leaving behind his breakfast.

Snarl climbed down the ridge, quiet and slow. Tuft had already gone into the den. Dusty rolls of tiny rock slid off the trail as he got near the opening. His arrival would be no secret.

He walked straight up to the den opening and poked his head in, adjusting his eyes to the semi-darkness. Tuft was lying down, staring up at him. She lifted her head when she saw him, but Snarl did not sense any anger or fear. She appeared calm.

Snarl looked outside, studied hiding spots, and tracked for any movements. He didn't see anything odd. A quiet morning in the canyon. He looked back at Tuft, and she lightly put her head down on her prone paws. Her eyes were half shut.

Snarl's tongue lay across his teeth, his mouth open, but he was not breathing hard. Yet, he could feel the tiredness in his body. He licked his face, closed his mouth, and went into the den.

He lay down next to Tuft and looked out the opening, as she seemed to be doing. He could feel her breathing because they had to be close together in such tight quarters. The pace of Tuft's breathing reminded Snarl of his mother, more than Spit. Tired, Snarl also put his head down on his paws. He turned his head to Tuft. Her eyes were shut. She was sound asleep.

This was a good place, after all.

ROCKS

Howl had brought deer remains to his pack a few nights before, stolen from a sleeping lion. He had snuck up and bit off a generous chunk of the deer, ran off, and the lion never knew he was there. His pack bowed their snouts to Howl when he returned. His rise among the males jumped another notch. Howl's cleverness and willingness to share did not go unnoticed. The two others from his pack joined him when he'd left to return to the carcass this morning. This was a dangerous hunt because of the lion. Howl would need help for a diversion.

Howl did not know the lion, who's deer meat he had stolen, was deaf. His escapade a few nights ago had given him a newfound courage.

After they arrived, Howl and the two coyotes took their time approaching the carcass. It was below the area where the lion rested. They could tell from a distance that the deer had already been picked clean. They stayed hiding behind a felled fir.

After a very long wait, the three coyotes whined at the lion, thinking they could get the lion to chase them and leave one of them to sneak in and see if there were any other morsels to steal. They got no reaction from the lion. The prone, still lion didn't respond to any noises they made.

The lion wasn't moving at all. Maybe it was playing dead to seize one of the coyotes in its teeth. Howl did not want to leave, not yet.

Howl remained still for a few more minutes. Suddenly, ravens filled the sky above the lion. They arrived from all kinds of positions in the trees. Howl hadn't noticed them earlier. He'll need to check the trees in the future.

In a strangely coordinated fall from the sky, spinning, almost crashing into each other, the birds landed one by one on the lion and began pecking away, wings flapping and beaks flinging fur in every direction.

Howl hadn't realized that the unmoving lion was dead. The ravens knew, though. Howl stood up from his crept position, unnoticed by the busy ravens, and inched forward. His pals joined him, spreading out as coyotes know how to do. Still unseen, when about ten yards away, Howl leaped in two bounds and landed squarely amid the birds. The birds instantly retreated and flew straight into the air as the two coyotes joined Howl standing upon a dead lion.

The lion was not located in a hiding spot where coyotes like to feast. The coyotes gripped chunks of the lion in their teeth, either by the skin or an appendage. They dragged the body, in chaotic fashion and with little progress, toward the bushes deep away from the rock ledge.

The ravens, however, had not given up. They flew back, crashing onto the backs of the coyotes. Then all manner of noises, a mix of raven croaks and coyote barks, sent everyone into utter confusion.

A coyote older than Howl, managed to bite into one of the ravens. Not with his back teeth, though. They were just nubbins, which fit his coyote name — Gummy. He was so surprised at his catch that his eyes were as big as Howl had ever seen them. The raven died quickly, but the other ravens seemed more energized, maybe because one of the coyotes had his mouth full.

Gummy trotted off with his raven. He would be going all the way back to the den. Howl and Tail, the third coyote, were having a dickens of a time moving the lion by themselves.

Howl felt a rock hit him in the side of his body. He couldn't believe it. Since when do ravens throw rocks? A second rock bounced off his snout. The rock came from a man off to Howl's right.

He saw him running at them, throwing one rock after the other.

Howl quickly tore off some meat of the lion's rump, shaking it loose with his head, and ran to follow Gummy. Tail, the fastest coyote in the pack, flew by Howl with a pile of fur in his jaws.

Howl didn't like men, and though the lion carcass was a loss, he had done well for himself and had a cache of meat to bring back. This would be a good sign for him in the pack.

He saw a rock bounce off the butt of Tail, who then ran even faster. That was the last he saw of either coyote until he arrived back at the den several minutes later. He howled like a warrior and got many nuzzles for bringing back meat to the den. Gummy had his raven, but Tail, who beat them both, had nothing but a mouth full of fur.

Even though Tail was the last to leave the carcass, he'd arrived first and looked like he'd run away.

Which they all did.

Walking Eagle heard the coyote yaps and the croaking of the ravens. Something was going on. He saw a falcon fly out of the area where he thought the noises came from. In a weird display of screeching, the falcon appeared to be telling Walking Eagle that something terrible was happening. He kept flying by him, swooping awfully close.

The old man still had some hurry in him, so he hiked up his arms and double-stepped to the ridge. He was headed in that direction anyway. The falcon left him, flying north.

As Walking Eagle entered the forest section of the ridge, he saw several black ravens and heard their croak-croak calls as they flapped at something below them. As he got closer, he could make out the source of the ravens' anger — three coyotes.

In a flurry of feathers, one of the coyotes grabbed a raven in his mouth. What a remarkable catch, Walking Eagle thought. Looked something like a dog catching a high-flying Frisbee. The ravens didn't let up, even with one of their own captured and killed by a coyote.

Walking Eagle continued toward the area, but not as fast. He saw one of the coyotes ripping some meat off a body on the ground. He stopped, horrified at the sight of the red meat. His brain focused on the body. It looked like it might be the back of a human.

He rolled his gun off his shoulder, quick, ready to take aim, and then immediately thought better of it. He held the rifle in his left hand, reached down, and grabbed a handful of pebble-sized rocks. He stuffed them in his jacket pocket and took off, running toward the commotion of coyotes and ravens. They hadn't yet seen him coming. In stride, he took one rock out of his pocket, took aim at the coyote with his back to him, and hit it on the belly. Still running, he took another rock, threw it, and hit the same coyote on the snout.

Mighty good aim, he said to himself, surprised, talking over his worry that the coyote had downed someone, maybe a hiker. The coyote he hit ripped off the last of some meat that he'd been working at, and that's when Walking Eagle saw the tail and leg of the body on the ground.

It was a lion. Walking Eagle was relieved it wasn't human but was sure it must be a lion he knew.

Two of the coyotes had run off, but one stood looking at him. He thought he might need the rifle, but before reaching for it, that one ran away too. For good measure, Walking Eagle threw one more rock at the coyotes, and lo and behold, it hit the mark.

"Strike three, and you're outta here!" he yelled at the coyotes.

The ravens then descended on the lion now that the coyotes were gone. Walking Eagle knew they didn't care much about him. Shoot, they didn't seem to even care that a coyote had snagged one of their flock, either.

Breathing hard, he sat down on a rock to catch his breath and calm his nerves. "Wow." He thought he'd seen a human being getting eaten by coyotes. He shook his head.

He raised a hand to the sky. "Thank you," he said. "I don't think I could have handled that."

After only a minute or two, wiping his face with his palms, Walking Eagle decided that he needed to see if the lion was one of the three who lived in this canyon, not far from here. The young male he'd been monitoring for the university belonged to the lion family — the male, his sister, and the mother. The male was the lion that Walking Eagle thought he had shot with a dart a few days back in the ranch's spring valley to the south. If he didn't get over to the carcass soon he wouldn't be able to tell.

Walking Eagle groaned as he stood up. The running and emotional tension had taken a toll. He shouted at the ravens as he moved toward the carcass, calling them names and throwing out insults. He didn't much care for ravens.

They ignored him. As he got closer, he tossed several handfuls of dirt at them, and they flew off to sit in some trees. He yelled at them some more, questioning their judgment at attacking three coyotes and yet quickly flying away from an old man who threw dirt.

When he knelt down at the torn-up lion body, he noticed the blotchy left ear right away. It was the male he knew, alright. He recognized the markings.

He checked for the white stripes he'd seen on the tranquilized lion, but there was no marking. Walking Eagle saw what looked like a gunshot exit wound on the side of the head below the ear. He turned the head and saw where a bullet had entered.

"Dang," he said, adding a few more unsavory words.

"Someone shot you and then left you?"

Walking Eagle knew about the April lion hunt season. Sometimes hunters accidentally came onto the Clayhall property. He'd never seen this before, though.

He ran all kinds of scenarios in his mind and then started looking for tracks. He saw that the body was dragged here to this short stretch of forest, from the south, near the top end of dry gulch canyon. It was easy to decipher the drag marks of the body over the ground. He followed them. The path of the dragged lion stopped about ten yards from where the lion body lay, on a ledge where the canyon began.

Blood splatters on an overhang of rocks showed where the lion must have taken the shot to the head. He recognized the area below. He was standing just above the lion's den. He fanned out from that point, looking for tracks from the hunter.

He moved his rifle to the crook of his arm. The other lions may be nearby. The idea of nervous lions nearby tingled the roots of what little hair he had left on his head.

He searched for hunter boot prints. Beyond the rock outcropping, all he could see were coyote and lion tracks. He backtracked a little farther and then saw the clue he needed. Dozens of imprints of dogs, in lengthy strides. They'd been running. He'd walked over them, following the drag of the lion's body.

He had assumed that the hunter had dragged the body and then gave up. But he didn't see any boot prints. He saw some coyote tracks and realized they'd moved the lion.

The dog prints were confusing, though. They didn't bunch up. If the dogs had cornered the lion here for the hunter to kill, they would have gathered together around here, where they might have pushed the lion back onto the rocks. The dog tracks just didn't connect to the kill area. They took off, down the ridge.

Walking Eagle knew that he'd find the hunters by tracking the dog prints backward from where they came rather than following them to where they were chasing. The tracks were pretty easy to follow. Had to be three or more dogs, which would mean what he knew to be true. A trained pack of dogs, owned by someone who knew how to corner or tree lions.

As he walked, Walking Eagle got more and more upset. First, a hunter comes on private land. Second, they kill a male and leave the body. He knew that only male lion licenses were available this season. Someone who kills a female might have a reason for leaving a body, though they'd broken all the rules, but why leave a male body?

He assumed that the tracks probably would head back from where he'd been, several hundred yards from National Forest property, but the dogs didn't come from that way. He was still thinking that the hunter had attempted to drag the dead lion to his truck. But the dog prints lead back to the canyon.

Walking Eagle had been hiking around for a while, and he considered heading back to his truck. He kept tracking, though, and followed the path of the dogs. He spat out a fling of insults and angry words, no longer aimed at the ravens but for a hunter that he wanted to find and give him a piece of his mind.

The day warmed up, but Walking Eagle zipped up his jacket. The gory scene of a hunted lion left as carrion for scavengers sent a cold chill through his stomach and chest.

He doubted that he would see the other lions. A killed lion near their den would ruin their sense of safety. They had probably run off. This was at least a day-old kill.

Still, he kept an eye out.

Tuft dreamed about walking to water and meat delivered to her. She saw Snarl at the den opening. He discovered her old home, and she looked up at him, wondering if he was bringing her food. She wasn't surprised to see him. He looked tired like she felt. He was such a calm lion, she thought.

Her eyelids were heavy, and she put her head down and tried to watch him. She began to drift off, smelling the fresh scent of kittens where her snout almost touched the ground.

She next felt Snarl's body lie down next to her. He moved very slowly, and she felt the warmth of his body.

She dreamed of the path she took from the trench to the stream and then to this den. She remembered the trees along the trails and how the roots of the tree trunks were shaped.

The water dripping off the rocks had tasted warm. Tuft felt a yawn coming, and she opened her mouth wide, taking in a slow gulp of air mixed with a memory of the taste of the water.

MEN

Claw hid with her kittens in a rocky crevice. She had crossed two canyons in as many days, deciding to head toward the sun rather than away or north.

She encountered more of the same men that forced her from the den near where she had birthed the boys.

She sought distance between them and her family, but they seemed to be everywhere. Fortunately, Claw learned to pick them out. She developed an image of them and their wolf-like animals. They were a new species for her to remember. Men and their hounds.

Another group had already chased her today. The hounds linked to the men kept finding her. They almost trapped her, but as they got close, the men and the hounds fell back, just like before. They let her go twice.

Claw rested long enough, sensing men's hounds might be following her yet again. She had to find a way to elude them. They might not let her go the next time. After the last canyon, which was quite large, she had found her way into a more level forest. She should be able to move more quickly and with better cover.

The kittens were hungry and were crying. Claw had to feed them, but she hadn't eaten. She needed to hunt. Claw tucked them into the crevice. It would have to do. They would wait for her, she hoped. She purred at them to be quiet.

She had no time to distract anyone following her, and instead, she focused all her attention on catching something to eat. She loped away, sniffing the ground, and in no time had found a track to some rabbits. She slunk off.

Spit lay on his back, his forelegs in the air. He was swatting at flies. He had been concentrating on noises since he had woken up from a nap. He was pretty good at it, too.

He could distinguish between the gnawing of a squirrel and the rustling of a rabbit. He could pick up the tweets of small birds as different from larger winged birds' caws, croaks, and screeches.

He'd also figured out that deer would walk if he just sat still. He didn't have to work so hard to find them. They were everywhere.

Most importantly, Spit was making connections between the noises and the quiet. Whenever he traveled, the sounds went quiet. If he stopped and waited, he could hear many different animal noises.

He was proud of himself.

He sat up and listened again. Not only was it a skill he enjoyed developing, but he felt the noises were supplying him with information.

Information that led him to food. He stared into the trees and then closed his eyes.

A new sound. A tiny cry. His memory banks flashed, he opened his eyes, and his ears perked up. He bounced up into a standing position and tracked for the noise. He turned his head slowly, twisting his ears, and got the direction. He skulked down from his resting spot and stalked, moving toward the cry.

The cry increased, and he crouched, moving more slowly, one leg at a time, adjusting his direction, he crawled through the forest toward the noise. After rounding through the trees, he pinpointed where the noise came from rather than just heading in a straight line. Rocks up ahead. The cry was very familiar. He couldn't place it, but he could remember that noise.

As he crept to the rocks, he peeked underneath a jutted-out point, and he saw two lion kittens. The kittens' eyes were shut. One was making the crying noise, the other breathing shallow.

Spit watched them and could see they were new kittens. He thought for a moment. Maybe he should eat them. He quickly backed up, uncertain of the idea. A whisper in his head said, "No."

That was new.

He smelled the air. A mother. They should have a mother someplace.

Maybe they belong to his mother. Perhaps his mother left them because she had these kittens. Spit peeked at them again. Is that why she left? The idea filled his head, and he ran around the area, sniffing the ground. Yes, he could smell another lion, but not like his mother. He couldn't be sure.

Then he heard barking. Wolves, or coyotes, off to his right. He glanced at the kittens. Between a desire to run away from the barking, or find the lion mother, he chose to remain engaged in the kitten's lives. He would head toward the barking.

Maybe the mother is over there. He ran, loping, on a rescue hunt. Maybe my mother is over there.

He ran toward the wolves. He had to see.

Walking Eagle concentrated on the dog prints, seeing them going several directions at the canyon bottom. He couldn't make sense of the patterns. Pawprints were everywhere. Three different kinds of human boot prints meant three men were working with the dogs.

He walked almost all the way down the canyon, forgetting until now that he'd have quite a ways to get back to his truck.

He calculated the time and knew he had better head back now. He could drive around to the canyon's bottom or come back tomorrow. If it rained, though, he wouldn't be able to follow the tracks very far.

That might not matter. The tracks were at least a day old already. All he'd found out was that hunters were in Clayhall's north canyon, and they must've come from the lower east road. That area was marked pretty well. They must have known they were trespassing.

He turned around, figuring he had to head back, but he kept an eye out for the lions. He was coming up from the bottom of the canyon. Not likely, but one could jump at him from above. He carried the rifle at the ready.

Several minutes later, more tired from the uphill climb, almost back to the top of the canyon, he heard a squeal, almost like a coyote. He moved over to a tree and listened to the sounds bouncing off the canyon walls. It sounded like it was coming from the north wall.

Were those coyotes coming back for him? He'd never heard of that before, but his nerves were on edge, anger spiked his emotions, and he was upset about hunters on the ranch's land. He didn't have a scope on the rifle. He had to use his eyes to see.

There was movement up on the ridge wall, to the north, halfway down the canyon. On the uphill end of the canyon, Walking Eagle was eye to eye with what looked like a puff of dust coming off the side of the canyon.

He couldn't make it out. Too far away.

He waited and then moved a little more quickly up into the end of the canyon, over by the creek for cover. That's when he walked by an animal cache, dug up, and spread out. It was another lion kill.

He heard that noise again, a coyote-like squeal from down the canyon, and he almost panicked. Walking Eagle's nerves had reached their limit. What was going on?

He performed a quick review of the dead lion but didn't want to be near it for long, with predators still picking through the carcass. He couldn't tell if the animal was one of the other lions, the sister or the mother, but he could be pretty sure. The color of the hair meant an older lion. Probably the mother.

His heart was beating fast. He tramped away from the creek, making noise and giving pause to any animals in the area, mainly squealing coyotes. He needed to get out of here and back to his truck.

Clayhall was going to get an earful. This did not look right. Walking Eagle was not having a good day.

Snarl was roused from his sleep by the sharp squealing sound of a coyote screaming in his ear. He hit his head on the den of the roof when he awakened, and Snarl crawled out of there as fast as possible, sending up a flurry of dust as he exited, then turned to face the animal still in the cave with Tuft.

Dust was in the air, and as it cleared, Tuft slowly came out of the den, sneezing away the dirt in the air. Snarl looked behind her, but the cave was empty.

She stood off to the canyon side of the trail while he kept looking around. She opened her mouth in a wide yawn, and the same squeal he'd hear a moment ago came out of her mouth.

Snarl jumped back, thinking maybe Tuft had swallowed a coyote whole. She just looked back at him and yawned again, but this time she didn't make any noise.

Snarl watched her closely, thinking maybe something was wrong, but she wasn't upset or anything. She rubbed her nose with her front paw and then walked right back into the den. He watched her circle inside and then lay down on her same spot.

Snarl sat on the trail and thought about things for a moment or two. He must have been mistaken. The noise was not a coyote after all. It was her.

After the dust had settled, he peeked in again, and she was sound asleep. He went back into the den, too, but he moved closer to the entrance this time. He liked being next to her quietly breathing body, but the next time she squealed, he didn't need it to blast into his right ear.

Grunt, the old owl, watched the hunters and their dogs moving through the forest. He flew from tree to tree, keeping an eye on them. Many times, the owl had followed hunters like these. Quite often, they had left food behind. Everything from the parts of an animal they had killed to small colorful presents with incredible tastes inside.

These fellas, however, behaved strangely. Twice this group had cornered the same mother lion. She was carrying two kittens. The hunters had let her go both times, holding back their dogs from a successful chase. Grunt was confused. No matter. He was looking for an opportunity to nab one of the kittens. He had followed the lion all morning, watching from high in the trees as the hunter's dogs would catch up to her.

After the second time they had cornered the mother lion, the hunters ended the chase. They held back their dogs and settled down. Grunt had to decide to follow the lion and hope for a kitten or snatch something left behind by the hunters.

He flitted about nervously on a perch, watching the lion race away. The high numbers of animals and men in the hunting party seemed the better decision. Especially when he saw them reach into their bodies and hand out morsels of some interesting-looking items to the dogs.

The lion was long gone. The old owl couldn't count but spied more hunters than dogs by owl reckoning. This was good news. The hunters owned the food. The dogs were more likely to eat everything they got. They exhibited an enormous amount of energy. The hunters sat on stumps of trees and rocks, dropping morsels in every direction.

Distracted for a minute by a black, pointy-eared squirrel, Grunt considered a meaty catch of squirrel rather than scavenging for crumbs. He watched the travels of the squirrel circling a nearby tree trunk as it climbed into the branches. The speed of the squirrel threw off the old owl's timing. Once in the upper limbs, Grunt wouldn't be able to get him.

The daytime light made the owl yawn. Grunt hadn't been very successful during the night and was still hungry. He swiveled his head back to the hunters, then sidestepped into the crossing of branches in the thicker outreaches of the pines in the tree where he stood. He blinked his eyes, realizing that he probably should rest. This would be an excellent place to sleep until dark. The crowd below should be gone by then, and he could check out what they may have left behind.

Just as his eyelids had settled halfway open, poised to drop shut completely, a flash of orange raced across the ground below him. He gripped the limb he was holding tighter and tracked the animal, imagining that it could be a lion.

He was right.

Into the midst of the hunters and dogs, the lion flew. It appeared to be startled by what it had just done, sliding to a stop on a stretch of dirt just a few feet from them. The hunters stood, and the dogs all turned to face the cougar. The lion's head pushed forward as it studied the animals. The owl believed this was a bold lion, surprising a strange herd of potential foods, selecting which one he should eat.

All of the hunters, four of them if he could count, raised sticks, pointing them at the lion. The dogs began barking simultaneously, and the lion leaped at the dog directly in front of him.

The old owl heard loud cracks, and the lion appeared to fly backward, landing in a dusty crash. The dogs jumped at the lion, nipping at it, but it didn't budge.

The owl was wide-awake now. Off to the right, not far from where he was perched, Grunt eyed the black squirrel again, clinging to the end of a branch, watching the scene below. This time the owl didn't hesitate.

Within seconds, he had the squirrel in his grip.

Better a squirrel to eat now than waiting for leftovers from the activity below.

He flew away from there.

Violence, death, and the eating of living things could just be coinci-
dence, an inevitability left from creation by nobody. The more radical
thought is death and killing result from creation gone awry. That is,
gone awry once creation ripped its willful connection to divinity, a
tightly woven relationship where all of creation once enjoyed a lovely
existence. It makes sense that the original creation included God as he
desired life. Gone awry, creation disconnected from the creator, infect-
ing life with corruption.

The creator, who allows creation to operate from free will, allows
such irrational results. Yet, God's free will design must play out in his
favor, for if God rules then creation must eventually follow. Consider,
then, the consequence of permanently rejecting God. Reject or follow.
What becomes of those who choose rejection?

Ultimately, all of creation, infected and hopefully repentant, re-
quire reparation and restoration. Don't they? God surely will redeem
the innocent, but what about the guilty who fail, yet yearn for God.
According to revelation's scriptures, if the texts are to be believed, God
has mercy on those who fail miserably, even repeatedly, when they
plead for mercy.

Creation is awry, indeed, yet who doesn't yearn for a loving God?
To no more be awry. Broken, pleading for a promise of repair. Who in
their right mind, not just cornered but sane, wouldn't plea for forgive-
ness, reparation, and restoration with God?

We hope never to break again. Repaired forever, for good.

Chapter Five

NEXT

*And God shall wipe away all tears from their eyes: and death shall be
no more, nor mourning, nor crying, nor sorrow shall be any more, for
the former things are passed away.*

—REVELATION 21:4

FOG

SPIT COULD HEAR SOMETHING, rather someone, calling him. The voice
didn't speak in words, of course. It spoke in a purred lion language. A
language that Spit could understand. It said, "Over here," as a lion grasps
that injunction. The utterance, or speech as a lion communicates, sounded
familiar, a voice between his ears, residing in the middle of his head. He
had heard the timbre and tone of sounds before, he was sure, but the voice
was clearer now.

"Come this way," it spoke again to him.

His eyes were open, but all he could see was a fog. Lit up from afar. Spit
looked behind him. There was no fog there. Just a second ago, he was facing
a group of animals he had never seen before. He had jumped at them, and
then in an instant, he was standing here.

Behind him, Spit could see something else, an undulating, shimmering space, an opening into a cave of darkness.

"Over here," the calm voice spoke again. Spit turned back to the light.
The sound was in the brightness, behind the fog.

He was standing up. Spit could feel the earth beneath his feet, soft
and firm at the same time. Then, a windy tingle whooshed through him,
like the warning pain on the skin beneath his fur in severe cold. This wind
passed through his entire body, feverish rather than cold. The tingle was
thorny, hot, and it came in waves. Waves of sharp, heated wind blew from
the direction of the light.

What had happened to the animals, he wondered? Where did this fog
come from?

Though the wind pushed at him, and thorns seemed to push through him, they did not force him away or make him step back, but slightly draw him forward. Flowing air enveloped him.

It hurt.

From the wind, he heard, "This way. Come this way." In a whisper, a motherly purr. He missed his mother. Spit moaned at the voice in the wind. The wind warned him to accept the prickly heat, telling him it would blister through him. The wind whispered for him to be courageous.

His paws trembled. Spit took a step into the fog, and another wave of wind shivered over and through his body, less painful this time, like cleansing steam from the hot pools he and his family visited. The wind was followed, once again, by the calm and soothing voice.

"It's alright. Don't be afraid."

Behind Spit, the darkness increased and began to pull at him. Not with an invitation like the wind. The black space bubbled in waves, without light.

The dark shrunk from the wind but a long, pawed black arm lunged at him, yanking with an invisible grip on his neck.

Spit heard harsh, coughing sounds from the darkness, strangled in rumbling thunder. The rumbles reached a roar. He listened for lions or some other loud howling animal. As Spit tried to separate the sounds into something familiar, he heard a mix of grating, hoarse commands to give into the pull upon his neck. The voices gurgled, emitting a stench which coated his throat.

He smelled meat. Spit's mouth watered, and his eyes searched for food.

The sounds began to morph into the shape of animals in the blackness, frightened, delicious-sounding voices, yelling, crying out to him, telling Spit to run away from the fog. Were they the animals he had just seen only moments ago in the forest?

"Run into the safety of the darkness," the cries choked in their strangled sounds. The smell of meat filled Spit's snout.

"No, this is the way," the fog lightly purred behind him, cooing to him.

Spit felt the flavorful pull into the darkness. He stood sideways, between the single purring voice and the roaring bountiful smells of flesh. The howls of many tiny screams sucked at him, drawing out the fog's warmth, replacing it with a stuffy, sultry fear.

He leaned into the darkness to find a familiar voice in the screams. A deer caught in the branch of a tree.

An elk with broken legs.

Twisting his head with difficulty, Spit turned to look back at the purr of the fog. It warmed him again, painfully cleansing away the hungry darkness he had just engaged.

Another wave of wind quickly followed and blew over and through him. The wind filled his body and satisfied him. Again, with pain, but a little less this time. He could feel the wind, even though half of him faced the darkness. The calm afterward left a thermal heat in every limb.

The warmth brushed his eyelids, not closing them in sleepiness, sharpening them instead with visions of forest and sky ahead.

His stomach growled, reminding him of hunger. The darkness hissed. Spit saw the first hint of color in the blackness — yellow teeth. The warm glow in the light, though, held Spit firmly, soothing his fur. The dark bubbled in angry response, and paws reached almost to his face.

Spit turned to the fog, and the wind abated, caressed him, and he rested for another wave. Mild strokes rolled through his spine, calming him. He stood between the worried, now shrinking, roaring of many voices and the one clear, quiet voice. He took another step into the fog to test the still purring of the light.

A long, intensive pulse of wind blasted through him again. Spit accepted it fully. The darkness washed away. He stepped further into the fog, peering at the light, blinking as he went.

He was dry-mouthed and hungry. He licked at the wisp of the fog lit up around him. Spit swallowed the fog, and it washed his throat clean. Thirst-quenching water came from the air. The voice continued to speak, urging him to walk into the brightness, which he did, while the roaring faded away. He felt his belly fill.

This is the way, Spit decided, enjoying the inviting light, the nourishing fog, and the warming wind. Then he spoke to it with his tongue.

"I am coming."

The falcon sat on a half-fallen tree, which had hung at an angle, dead and dried out for a very long time. It leaned against a weary Spruce, burdened by dead weight. The fallen tree was broken above the roots, held by the Spruce, pointing toward the horizon.

Pikes Beak took his meals near the top, on a bowed cup of branches he had piled long ago into his favorite resting spot. He finished off the last of a dead prairie dog that the elk had trampled for him.

He tore it to shreds, ripped apart with his beak while held in his feet. The shredding made the eating easier.

The falcon screeched another thank you to the elk, stretching out his neck. He lifted his wings into a wide arc. Indeed, they recognized his gratefulness, he thought to himself. Pikes Beak shoved what was left of skin and bones out of his perch, and it fell lightly to the forest floor.

The wind blew hard today, a perfect time for gliding. The falcon sat on his feet in the carefully placed bows of his perch, closed his eyes, and said to the air that he needed a little more time to enjoy the meal in his belly.

He lifted his wings to carefully place himself facing into the wind, and a sudden gust lifted him off the dead tree, took him up into the air, and flew him where he did not want to go.

Darkness fell quickly. Walking Eagle had to stop and rest. He sat on his heels, elbows rested at his knees. His heart was pounding. Afraid, he wrapped his arms around his sore chest.

The truck was parked far from where he sat. There was no moon. Darkness had quickly blanketed the view of the horizon around him. Every way he looked was the same.

He did not know the location of the stars to project a way to the truck, but it didn't matter. According to his last reckoning, the light fog which filled the air was rolling in from the north. All helpful constellations were blocked. Walking Eagle only had the wind to help him.

The mist began to thicken. He squared his body in one direction because north would soon get twirled away. The worried ranger couldn't stand and walk. Not now. Upright put too much pressure on the heart. Walking Eagle realized he was close to being lost. He reckoned the road was to the north. A trail to his east, one he knew well, would send him back up north. He cheated his northern plans with little moves heading him to the east. If he was wrong, heading south or west instead, then he'd be spending the night in this painful condition.

The fog already quit cooperating. It seemed to be rolling from every side. He no longer knew which way to go.

Walking Eagle wondered what he should do. His heart was calming down when he stayed still, so he decided to wait. Maybe the heart would get back to normal. This had happened before, but not with this intensity. He sat and took deep breaths.

His gun had been misplaced some ways back when he grasped at his chest in pain. He reached to find it, but that activity could further confuse his direction. The darkness and the fog crept in faster. His heart started pounding again, and the pain increased. He stopped moving, sat back on his heels, and rested his arms again upon his knees.

"Oh boy," he said, clutching his chest tightly. He clenched his teeth and tried to calm himself by taking deep breaths and exhaling slowly.

"Whew," he said each time he let out the air.

OSCAR

Oscar sat on his couch. He could see his food bowl from there. Also, Oscar could see out the window with a slight turn of his head. Headlights from all kinds of vehicles passed by, but none were from the truck he knew so well.

When darkness came, Oscar was outside in the backyard. Dark meant it was time to get his supper. Supper was in the kitchen. He twisted the back doorknob with his paw and pushed his way into the house, then directly to his bowl. It was empty, so he trotted over to the couch in the front room to wait.

His long ears lightly touched his cheeks. Oscar's front paws hung over the back seat edge. One of his hind legs had dropped, casually touching the carpeted floor.

Another set of lights.

No, that's not Randy's truck.

He took another glance at his bowl. Still empty.

Far behind the main herd, two bull elk wandered into the prairie from the edge of the forest. The darkness and fog would keep them undercover, they figured. They were forced to walk a great distance behind the herd. The primary bull of their herd did not like them. Two younger bulls were threats to his dominance. The old bull never seemed to tire. The young elk breathed hard, exhausted. The cagey, determined elk chased them every chance he got.

The two bachelors stuck together to fight off lions, wolves, and coyotes. They already outran a couple of lions just a while ago. The lions would follow them, they knew. The fog would give the two elk a chance to move with the herd, escaping both lions and staying clear of the big, angry bull elk.

Fog blew into their nostrils, and they exhaled spiraling flows of their cold breath. One after the other, they stepped into the prairie, heading north.

After talking with Uncle Jonas, Randy touched "end" on his cellphone and stared at it. His uncle had called him and asked what he was doing this evening. That had never happened before.

Randy had plans in Castle Rock. He had to go shopping for himself and Oscar. His fridge was empty. His plans weren't that important, though.

What did Uncle Jonas want? He had to go. He owed his uncle.

The shopping could be done anytime. Randy would just get something at a burger joint. He could gobble down the burger on the way to meet up with his uncle. Oscar might be a problem. So, no burger. He'd stop at the Safeway and get one of their cheap sandwiches and some dog food. He'd pick up Oscar and take him. Kind of half shopping, he grunted to himself.

His uncle said to bring the dog. Curious request.

"Oh, and hurry," were his final words to Randy.

Snarl started out just before dark. Tuft was following him. Her retracing business slowed him down. Snarl put up with it. She moved without making noise, and that was more than Spit had ever done. He liked having her with him.

Paying attention to Tuft and her lowered nose to the ground had distracted Snarl, though. They practically bumped into two elk coming upwind through the forest above the ridge the lions now called home. The elk were only a tree length away when they stopped and checked each other out. The elk flinched first and leaped back in the direction from where they came.

Tuft took off at the same instant that Snarl charged into the trees. The elk would be much faster than the lions, so they needed to find a way to separate one from the other. Then, they would need to corner the slowest one — up against a rock wall, a cliff, or something like that.

Snarl had an untested circular map of the canyon in his memory. The elk were heading alongside the canyon toward the sunset. He and Tuft would get just one chance to trap an elk at the cliff edge before they ran out of canyon narrows. That's where the canyon met the forest, and the cliff wall disappeared. Bull elk can run fast and escape easily into the woods. Snarl didn't think they could catch them in time.

Sure enough, the elk cleared the canyon way before the lion's bursts of speed ran dry. They went into the deeper forest, keeping a pace the lions could not maintain.

Tuft only stopped because Snarl did. She looked back at him, waiting for a sign. She'd done this before, he realized. She had good trapping skills. She didn't hesitate at all. She looked in the direction of the distant elk and back at him.

Snarl turned away and headed north from the canyon into the trees. He had an idea that the elk might come back this way, not along the canyon. The elk probably still intended to travel in the same direction. They might circle back.

Tuft followed.

They walked slowly, lightly padding the ground with their feet as they moved. Tuft periodically looked over at Snarl. He could see her watching him. Snarl looked for a rise of sorts in the forest, someplace where they could see toward the direction the elk would return.

Darkness slowly descended upon them. Snarl smelled fog in the air. That would be good for him and Tuft. The elk would only have the ground to follow. He and Tuft weren't going to be moving at all. They should have the advantage.

The city lights concealed the night's moonless dark when Randy got to the road leading past the ranch's gate. The drive from Castle Rock to his uncle's house wasn't long. His uncle lived about a mile west of the ranch entrance, one of the biggest landholdings in the county.

Randy and his Uncle Jonas had only recently reconciled. After turning eighteen years old, Randy graduated from high school but refused to go off to college like his mom and dad had expected. His uncle took his dad's side. Jacob, Randy's dad, and Jonas eventually accepted the boy wasn't going to any more schools. Worried about Randy's opportunities, though, Uncle Jonas had offered him a full-time job on the ranch.

Randy turned his uncle down, not interested in working on a mountain property, he said. That was a lie. Randy felt he needed to "pay his dues" laboring in a place where he could live an independent life. Uncle Jonas' job was perfect, but he'd still be just a kid. Randy liked hunting, working on his truck, and getting paid by the hour at an entry-level job would teach him important things.

Randy read what he wanted to read, spent his spare time anyway he liked, ate meals he bought with his own money, or cooked up by himself. He didn't have plans beyond low-paying retail jobs since he was unsure about the future. He had plenty of time.

Randy's father, Jacob, was dumbfounded. Uncle Jonas was disappointed. Randy wished they understood that he simply wanted to postpone lifetime decisions for as long as possible.

To appease his son, Randy's father offered him a place to live, a rundown house in Castle Rock. He could stay there for no cost if he upgraded the property over the next year. Jacob would sell the property and split the profits with his son. Randy agreed, breaking his desire for fully independent living. Still, he'd earn his way, save rent with renovation labor, and get his dad and uncle off his back.

Uncle Jonas relented to Randy's decision, and offered his land to the young man whenever he wanted to get out with his dog. He'd already arranged a time, which came up just a few days ago. He allowed Randy to take Oscar and some young hunting dogs in training to hunt on the Clayhall Ranch. Randy worked off and on at a breeding kennel where he'd gotten Oscar many years earlier.

Any chance at hunting was a good time. Well, maybe not as yesterday's lion hunt had gone. However, running around and showing off to his friends capped off a fine day.

Now, Randy owed his uncle at least an evening. Randy didn't know what his uncle wanted, but he'd go.

Oscar sat in the front of the truck with his seat belt on. Randy was sure Oscar was the only dog in the universe who wore a seat belt. Oscar's nose prints were all over the passenger side window. He'd eaten his food in the truck right away, then climbed into the seat. The empty bowl sat on the truck floor mat below him.

The dog's regal poses, and periodic sideways glances, reminded Randy of his dad. He chuckled at that, wondering if he would ever let that slip out.

His thoughts shifted back to his uncle. Hopefully, he wouldn't talk about either school or a job at the ranch. Uncle Jonas's voice resembled his dad's, which had the same tense worrying sound on the cell call. Neither his dad or uncle said much, especially over the phone.

"I need you out here and bring your dog," he'd said. "Oh, and hurry."

Randy was sure he would be getting a lecture or some cockamamie story that his uncle and dad had conjured up. He looked at Oscar. Maybe Oscar was in on it.

"So, what do you and Uncle Jonas have up your sleeves?"

Oscar gave him a passing glance.

"Tight-lipped as always," Randy said.

ELK HOOVES

Red followed the elk herd at a distance. He had been lucky once to find an elk carcass left behind a few weeks ago, one abandoned by larger predators who had brought the animal down. Red had been tracking this herd since he finished the last of his lion meat earlier in the day. The elk walked from below the late sun out to the open prairie, moving slowly but methodically.

The elk's long legs prevented Red from getting too close. He followed along just inside the forest edge, his tail floating out straight behind him. The idea to follow them was not to quell hunger. He wasn't hungry. He saw elk and felt an urge to walk with them. Curiosity was essential to Red. It usually led to something good.

While he would like to lounge around, enjoy the scenery, and ponder things, his inquisitive character, always eager to skulk and watch, set Red into action.

He followed the elk.

Walking Eagle crawled. His heart calmed somewhat when on his hands and knees. Sitting, he grew cold. He needed to move. Standing would not work.

So, he crawled.

In the thickened fog, he tried to plod in just one direction. The wet air muffled distant noises, so Walking Eagle became alarmed at what sounded like two huffing moose. They had to be close. He couldn't see them until they almost stepped on him. Two tall, leggy animals lumbered by within inches. They either didn't notice him or didn't care.

Walking Eagle remained still as he could in his crawling position as they passed by him, head down and hands on the back of his neck. They smelled of wet hair and mossy breath. He felt the legs of one brush against his left hip, and then they were gone, pounding ahead as if he wasn't even there.

Walking Eagle knew their huge feet would have left deep imprints in the grassy plain. He reached to his left and felt the ground. The double crescent dips in the earth were right there. But they weren't big, like moose. They were elk.

Walking Eagle shook his head in amazement at his good fortune. He didn't realize until now the unlikely chance of this happening. These elk were laggards, following behind a herd he knew. Their sound and smell made him think of moose for some reason. Earlier in the day, an elk herd had traveled within a few feet of his truck, heading into national forest land. His vehicle was parked right there. These elk must be migrating too, walking very near his truck.

The elk tracks should be easy to follow, even in the fog. Walking Eagle's head, just inches above the ground, couldn't see anything. He had no light, just a faint luster in the starlit fog. He had to feel for their footprints, two large divots about the size of his hand.

Slow in the foggy dark, but mostly because his heart wasn't keen on speedy exertion, he crawled with the elk path. He had no idea how far from the truck he was nor how much energy he could maintain. The prairie, though, was somewhat flat. He wouldn't have to climb over large boulders.

After what seemed like a mile of crawling but may have only been a few hundred feet, Walking Eagle's left leg cramped. He stopped and stretched his leg. In the process of stretching, he heard something hit the ground near his belly.

He sat upon his heels and felt around his knees, touched it, and knew it right away. His cell phone.

"Oh my God!" he shouted. All along, he had his cell phone! How could he not have remembered that. "You're such an idiot!" Walking Eagle shouted.

He needed to call for help. He pressed the power button at the top of the phone, which wasn't easy to find. He was not familiar with it. It was only for emergencies. This was an emergency, and he'd not planned for it.

"What were you thinking?"

It powered on. The phone lit up like a flashlight. "Yes," Walking Eagle shouted. He hadn't thought of that until it lit up the whole area where he sat.

Several icons showed up, but his sight was blurry. Even with its bright light, he couldn't tell one icon app from another. He could only see rounded, blurred colors. "Uh oh," he thought. His sight had deteriorated. That, along with a pained chest, must mean something dangerous was happening to his body.

Walking Eagle remembered that a green button was the one to make calls. He pressed what he thought might be it. Several rows of words showed up. He couldn't make them out but assumed they were his "favorites." His daughter had put them in. The top one was set up as Clayhall's phone, so he touched it, then held it to his ear.

Nothing. No ring. No beep-beep for a busy signal. Nothing.

He was angry with himself. Maybe there was no reception here, but more likely, he simply didn't know how to use the phone. He lightly tapped the phone on his forehead, chastising his lack of attention to the new-fangled thing.

He was getting dizzy. His heart began to hurt again. He held the phone in his left hand, still on, and lowered his head, back down on his hands and knees. That was better. The blood rushed to his head. He was getting colder, though. The temperature was dropping.

Walking Eagle held the phone between two fingers, pointing it toward his other hand as he started crawling again. The light from the phone was a big help. He could easily see the tracks of the elk, now. He began trudging along again on his knees. Not that he could go much faster, but the light was a welcome friend.

Pikes Beak flew just above the fog, thinking this night was a colossal waste. He couldn't see anything down there. He wasn't even sure if bats would fly in this stuff.

He was still hungry, so he considered heading to the ground and hopping around. He'd been lucky before.

Lifting his wings, Pikes Beak shifted his body into the slight wind pushing the fog, his bowed legs angled to touch the ground if he came in too quickly.

He heard elk huffing in the fog, and it lifted his heart. He listened for where they had been rather than where they were going. There might be another fortunate, unintentional elk-squashing of an unwitting prey.

Randy was nervous. His uncle asked him to drive the ranch's new Ram truck. The vehicle was decked out with every feature. Randy thought the coolest ones were the lights on top of the cab. Jonas had them installed for aiming lights at night. Well, this was a night where they could use them.

His uncle didn't want to talk about school or jobs. He needed help locating the retired forest ranger that worked for him. The fellow's name was Andrew McDermott, but his uncle said he used his Indian name most of the time — Walking Eagle.

Randy and Oscar had met him once. Mr. McDermott had dropped his right hand, and Oscar had walked right up to him, letting the man rub the back of his head.

Uncle Jonas sat in the back seat. Becky McDermott sat up front in the passenger seat. She insisted on coming, and Jonas insisted she sit up front to see. Her young eyes were better than the old man's, and besides, she needed to be busy doing something. Becky was Walking Eagle's daughter, a 17-year-old girl who went to Randy's old high school.

Oscar was relegated to the seat directly behind Randy, next to Jonas. A blanket sat under him. He put up a bit of a fuss about not sitting up front, but Randy was insistent. Oscar licked Randy's arm to confirm he understood.

"He didn't call either you or me, Mr. Clayhall," Becky said. "He's several hours late. I'm worried."

"I know," Jonas said. "My nephew is good in the mountains. Oscar has met your dad, too. We'll find him."

Randy suggested going back to get some more dogs. But when he brought up going back to town, Becky thought the idea of a lion-hunting dog pack looking for her dad in the dark didn't sound right, and the extra time would drive her crazy.

Mrs. McDermott stayed at home. She was already in a fright and would be more trouble than help.

Jonas had all the lights on the truck beaming, plus he brought flashlights, blankets, guns, Oscar, and the Search and Rescue team waiting for a "go" in town if the three of them were unsuccessful. Made sense to just go with the four of them at this point.

"He's not very good with that phone. Maybe his car broke down, and he's walking to the ranch," Becky said, talking fast and searching for possible reasons for her dad being missing. She was getting more worried by the minute.

Heading up the north road was a good idea, Randy thought. Fortunately, Mr. McDermott was said to be a man of habit. Uncle Jonas told Randy that he made a complete property circle at the end of each day. He came down this road, honked and waved at the ranch as he passed by and went out the gate to go home.

"Does he go off the road with his truck?" Randy asked, thinking maybe they should have been looking off to the sides of the road. They'd gone about half a mile already.

"Not usually," Uncle Jonas said, considering the thought. McDermott liked to walk off the road rather than drive. "Let's take the road all the way around first, and then we'll come back and look closer to our left and right."

The next few minutes were uncomfortably quiet. At least it was a clear night, thought Randy. Then, a mile before the road rounded to head west along the National Forest edge of the property, they saw the fog.

"Oh no," said Becky. "Slow down. I can't see very far now." It rolled upon them in seconds.

Uncle Jonas reached from the back seat and flipped the switch for the tracking lights on the top of the truck. Just as he did so, the fog lit up so brightly that Randy came to a complete stop.

"Wow," Randy shouted, pressing his foot even harder on the brake, even though he was stopped. The fog was flowing by them at a slow speed, but just enough to give him the feeling that the truck was still moving.

Then, a loud bang reverberated inside the cab. A bird hit the windshield head-on. The bird's wide wingspan spread over the whole window. Its head crunched sideways.

"Holy cow!" Uncle Jonas shouted from the back seat. Oscar barked but stopped when Randy hushed him.

Uncle Jonas opened the truck's back door and ran around to the front of the vehicle. The bird's sizeable legs were hanging below the wipers, appearing to brace him as he stood on the hood. Uncle Jonas could tell this was an unusually old falcon, both because of its size and the coloring of the feathers. It was not moving. Between its legs sat a cellphone, lit up, facing into the cab.

"That's dad's phone!" yelled Becky from inside the truck.

SACRIFICED

Snarl and Tuft sat on their spot, a lofty, hilly rise in the forest. They watched the fog roll into the prairie. Just across the top layer of fog only the stars lit the clear sky above. The last sliver of the moon was gone.

Snarl suspected that the elk had gone into the prairie below the fog. They'd been sitting for some time. He looked over at Tuft. She was watching him, waiting for him.

Snarl's mother was a good hunter. He stared at Tuft but did not see the look of his mother's hunting eyes. He watched Tuft join him in the race after the elk. She balanced her running against his, widening their attack. The decisions, though, were all his. When he slowed, she slowed. When he went faster, she went faster. She added to his options, though. Tuft seemed to know precisely what Snarl was doing. Snarl couldn't figure that out. Though they hadn't yet taken down a meal, the idea of the two of them hunting together gave Snarl confidence he enjoyed thinking about.

Tuft scooted closer to Snarl like they were together in the den. She was smaller than Snarl by one-third and much skinnier. Her body was not as warm as his, and Tuft absorbed his heat. She was close enough to put her head down on his paws, which she did, just underneath his head. Tuft purred, warming her jaw on his front feet.

They watched the night sky move as the stars leaned into the horizon where the sun had gone down. The deep black darkness behind the starlight contrasted with the billowy fog below them.

Snarl blinked and rested his head upon the space between Tuft's ears and felt her brow warming under his jaw.

When Snarl's mother went away, he was ready to accept it. She had already stopped watching him. Nothing he did for her recreated that gaze. He missed her attention but now she was gone. Tuft entered his life at just the right time. He was delighted at the goodness of it.

A light wind blew wafts of the fog upward, wisps of wet air reaching towards Snarl's nostrils. His exhales blew white breath, meeting up with the mist.

The shared warmth with Tuft welled up another sense in Snarl. This was different from both his brother's expectations and the attention from his mother. He'd spent his whole life with them, and now they were gone. Tuft offered a new, unexpected set of expectations and attention. It felt right.

Tuft's ears twitched beneath Snarl's jaw, flickering each time the chirping of crickets reached a crescendo.

Snarl had willingly provided for Spit over the winter as their mother seemed to disintegrate. Nonetheless, he had to leave him behind. Giving up that responsibility left Snarl uneasy, but he had no better choice.

The kinship with Tuft was exciting. So quickly, they seemed to share more than just eating and protection. He felt a new need for her presence rather than an expectation or need for attention. The sense of being with her was unique.

A wisp of fog lifted up from the white blanket over the prairie, and Snarl felt his brother's presence.

Snarl lifted his head to look. Tuft purred, and he could feel her body shiver in the cold. He put his head back on hers. He blinked at the fog, hoping somehow that his brother was all right.

He hoped the same was true for his mother.

Red spent the evening walking and discovering nothing of significance to eat. The elk were gone. He reached the end of his territory, signified by a hesitance in his steps over fading familiar ground cover and landscape. A few bugs, some interesting pieces of dung, and not much else. He turned around, traipsing on the tips of his paws beneath the fog that rolled overhead.

The fog's thin light left a dim, shadowy image of a roundabout trail Red knew back to his den. His night vision quickly translated the terrain from rock against dirt against brush into lines against circles against sharp corners. His nose worked out the rest, and in no time, he was bouncing along on the toe tips of his paws, headed back home.

With his head's mapping switched into shadow vision, Red didn't translate correctly an odd light hopping into his image on the right. His instinctual reaction to jump left of the bouncing light bumped Red head-to-head into a crawling beast that seemed to also be following the light.

Red held up his left paw to fling at the beast's head, his claws extended, while he simultaneously watched the light go from the ground into the air. Red's mouth opened wide as his head raised.

In a flash of wind, Red recognized a falcon's wing and the feathery legs of Pikes Beak. He knew that old falcon! Behind the falcon's shriek, Red heard also the singing man's voice. Red's thoughts were spinning about delicious round brown eggs, dangerous falcon claws, a bouncing light in the wind, and the body of the man rising just in front of him.

Red found himself standing on his hind legs, his left paw in the air, claws armed, wide-eyed, and pretty much dazed by the whole adventure. The light took off into the sky, and Red decided to take off, too. He dropped to all fours and burst away, barely touching the ground as he zoomed into the fog.

Walking Eagle had made much better progress with the light in his hand as he crawled across the elk tracks toward what he hoped would be the road and his truck. He must be getting close. The elk tracks continued unabated, plodding forward in what Walking Eagle thought should be north.

His heart still pained him, but the sharpness had settled down to a steady heaviness in his chest. The crawling didn't appear to be putting any stress on his heart that wasn't already there. The fog's cooling might be a good thing, he thought, or wished, or more probably was just making up.

"See," he said. "Listen to yourself, Doctor McDermott. You've got a great bedside manner."

He wished he was in his bed.

The pattern of the moving light calmed him as he crawled. The phone's cadence, up and down, while moving with his hands soothed him in this most ridiculous of situations. He couldn't remember ever crawling across a prairie in the fog, much less anywhere else.

Just as he was getting comfortable with his circumstance, he bumped his head into a fox.

Apparently, the fox was just as surprised as he was. It held up a paw to him, Walking Eagle thought, as if the fox were saying, "Hey, what are you doing here?"

Walking Eagle sat back on his heels, shone the light on the fox, and it stood up on its hind legs. "Hey, I know you!" he yelled at the fox.

"You want the light?" he asked his egg-eating friend. Walking Eagle stood up, holding the light high in the air, away from the fox.

From out of nowhere, Walking Eagle felt a sharp scrape against his raised hand, jerked his head up, and caught the sight of an enormous falcon grasping at the phone with his left talon. It squeezed his knuckles with the other talon, cutting into his hand.

"Owww!" Walking Eagle screamed. The falcon screeched, pulled the phone away, then took off with it, straight up into the sky of fog.

"Oh my God!" He watched the disappearing beacon as his phone flew away with the falcon.

Walking Eagle brought down his hand, cut in jagged slices by the falcon, and grasped it in his other hand. His heart raced just like before, and he dropped back down to his knees.

The fox was gone. The falcon was gone. His phone was gone.

"What in holy crap is going on?" he shouted. "Yes, Lord, I'm talking to you!"

He was breathing rapidly and felt himself sinking into the darkness around him. His confidence wilted. He wasn't angry and even scared. Not really. He was baffled.

Still crouched, resting his butt on his heels, Walking Eagle dropped his head, grasping not only his chest but also his injured hand. He sat rocking, back and forth, then began several slow breaths.

"Our Father, ..." he prayed, over and over. Every so often, he'd exaggerate a phrase, raising and lowering his voice into the fog. "In heaven," he shouted, a little louder. "On earth, as it is in heaven," he sighed.

He didn't feel able to crawl anymore. He had to hold his hand. It was bleeding.

Several minutes went by. Walking Eagle didn't know how long he sat there as he rocked himself back and forth, both to keep warm and to keep from worry. Even though the situation seemed bleak, the rocking and praying finally calmed him down.

"OK, Lord. What next?"

Then, not something he expected.

"Be still, my soul: the Lord is on thy side," rang out in the fog. There was music in the air! It was a church selection of songs he'd never been able to get working on the phone.

"Be still, my soul: thy best, thy heavenly friend through thorny ways leads to a joyful end . . . "

Prance and her fawn cuddled under a tree. The herd had lost a fawn that wandered off. They saw the lion that took it, then ran through the canyon to a prairie to escape the lion's territory. They'd been bunked down here for one night. Sharp Eyes had successfully led them to water, not far from where a human den was located. They had been down the canyons this way before. Being around men was not a good idea to Prance. But here they were.

Fog settled in. Sharp Eyes walked their perimeter and took a spot opposite of Prance, far to the other end of the herd. She watched him, wondering why he never located himself near her and the fawn that belonged to him.

She was not overly cautious, she thought. The wandering fawn was proof of that. She'd bleated warnings to no avail. Sharp Eyes might be getting too old. Maybe the buck is leaving me over here as the next one to get taken. Maybe another male will come. That was just fine with Prance. Better to get with a younger buck anyway. Surely, better than a lion.

Prance looked at the large group, wondering if safety in numbers eventually worked against her. Perhaps this herd was too large.

Decisions weren't something she planned out. The ideas just popped into her head. She believed ideas happened to protect her and keep her alive. And, her fawn.

Bucks were vital. They fought. They found food and water. They were supposed to find shelter. They were supposed to protect the fawns.

She turned and looked outside of the herd rather than inside. She would have to keep a watch if Sharp Eyes wouldn't.

Becky held the phone in her hands. It had been turned on. The screen wasn't set to make a call but to play music. She wasn't sure what that meant, other than her father decided he wanted to listen to music rather than call them.

"My dad's totally ludicrous," she spat out.

She looked for the Bluetooth connection setting to see if it was turned on. No. She turned it on and then returned to the music.

"What are you doing?" Randy asked her.

"Leave me alone," she said while she poked at the phone. She was trembling.

Jonas gently lifted the falcon off the windshield, holding it by the wingtips. He walked to the side of the road and placed the dead but magnificent animal on the ground.

Oscar barked from inside the truck. Randy shouted at him to be quiet, more loudly than regular conversations with his dog. Oscar looked at him, and Randy shrugged his shoulders as a limp apology.

Jonas looked over at the two teenagers, standing in the glare of the headlights. He had turned off the rooftop searchlights. The fog too quickly sucked up the light. It didn't seem to help their view at all.

Randy crossed his arms to warm them, looking down the road. "We should keep going," he said.

"I know, I know!" Becky yelled, but she had an idea.

"Let's all calm down," Uncle Jonas said, walking up to the two of them. "Back in the truck. Do you want me to drive, Randy?"

"No," Randy said. He turned away from Becky, walked to the truck, got in the back seat, and sat next to Oscar, who had started barking again. Randy gently grabbed the skin on the back of his neck, and Oscar stopped.

"OK. OK. I've got the Bluetooth running now," Becky said, getting into the front seat. "Roll down your windows. If dad left the speakers plugged into the cigarette lighter, we should be able to hear music coming from his truck."

Randy pushed the button on his door, and the window slid down. He nodded a couple times before saying, "Good idea. That's actually pretty clever."

"No duh," Becky said, and then quickly added in a quieter voice, "Thanks."

Uncle Jonas turned on the searchlights again and had Randy run them, one to the left and the other to the right of the road as they drove.

"Let's go find your dad, Becky," Jonas said, heading out slowly.

Pikes Beak was flying in a fog, though not like he knew. He had been looking into the mist just a moment ago and saw some light, but then this place where he was flying simply "happened." In an instant a whole new world appeared around him.

A flat light glowed behind the fog in front of him. The light was not coming at him but urging him forward. He was gliding, easily floating without effort, on a wind that warmed his entire body. He stretched his arms, and the fog began to clear up. Pikes Beak thought the fog might not be clearing. It may just be his eyes clearing up.

The light then filled up everywhere around him, embracing him. His eyes searched for something familiar. He was still gliding, slowly, wafting in the warming wind. The pleasant feeling grew to a crescendo as the light went from a golden to the whitest white he had ever seen.

He didn't burst into the light or fall into it. He was flying in it.

He heard a beckoning to "Come." The sound came from the full space of light in front of him, not just a part of it. He flew to the bright whiteness, curious, trusting, unafraid.

Just as the burst of light fully arrived, it changed into a sky, a blaring blue with billows of clouds everywhere. He sensed he'd had flown out one of these clouds and was now in the warmest, sweetest smelling air. The air filled him, nourished him.

He drank as he flew.

He saw more birds. Not just more, but hordes of birds. Flocks of birds beyond what could ever be. They were all flying, dipping and diving, gliding, and drinking up the atmosphere.

Their shrieks were not sharp. More sing-song. Pikes Beak called to them. Many heard him, sliding into his draft, gliding along with him. They looked over at him, all sorts of birds. Pikes Beak recognized only a few of the species. Some were huge, but none seemed to be afraid. Not afraid of him or the enormous birds all around them.

He shrieked to warn them that he was dangerous. They didn't seem to know. The noise that came out of his beak surprised him. He didn't shriek. He was singing, just like them.

He shrieked again, but his voice twittered. The sound was sweet, and the other birds warbled back, rocking their heads as they sang, jockeying for position to wave their wings at him.

His shrieks had always scraped at his throat. All noise felt that way to him. Shrieks of warning, shrieks of anger. This new soft warbling caressed his throat, exciting him to make even more noise.

He spun to catch a glimpse of all the birds around him, and he saw some with berries. He turned and flew upside down, something new for him. A bird, he thought a hawk, though quite large, slowed just above him with a berry in its mouth. It dropped the berry to him, and Pikes Beak grabbed it from midair.

He bit into the berry, and the taste drained into him like sweet water flowing from a rock. He sang in delight, and the hawk flew by him, raised his eyebrows to acknowledge him, and dove down.

Pikes Beak fell into the nourishing warm air, still tasting the amazing berry, and wondered what the hawk would show him.

Oscar wanted to get the falcon and bring it to the truck. He thought Randy would like him to do that. He pulled at the seat belt, but Randy told him to stay. Then everyone got back in the truck.

The falcon lay there by the side of the road. Oscar couldn't understand why they left him there. Barking at Randy about the falcon didn't have any effect. Randy sat next to him and pulled lightly on his neck.

Oscar looked at Randy and stopped barking. The falcon wanted to come into the truck. It tried awfully hard. When it hit the windshield, Oscar saw the light go out in its eyes.

Maybe he wanted to attack the girl in the front seat. Randy seemed worried about her. Oscar looked at Randy again, staring at the back of the girl's head. OK, then. We'll protect the girl from falcons. Maybe from other animals, too. Point made. No falcons in the truck. Oscar would remember that.

They found Walking Eagle rather quickly. First, they spied the truck, and then Oscar found him.

Becky joined her father after getting him into his truck to check out his injuries. He said he felt fine, but it took some time to wrap his hand correctly. Fortunately, Jonas had a brand-new First Aid Kit. They were heading to the hospital as soon as Jonas could talk Walking Eagle out of driving.

Oscar found him quickly because Walking Eagle was singing. Randy and Becky ran after Oscar and spotted him not that far off the road, licking her dad's face.

They saw Walking Eagle's truck about a mile farther from where the falcon brought them the phone. That's what Walking Eagle said about the falcon, anyway.

"The falcon brought you the phone to rescue me. "Be still my soul," was just a comical choice," he explained, practically giggling.

Becky smirked, but her dad wasn't making any sense at all. His explanations about what happened were a total jumble of elk "being late to the party," and suspiciously dead lions, and so on. Oh, and a shocked fox.

"If I had another egg, maybe the fox could've saved me," came out right after he was upset to find out the falcon had died.

"What fox?" Randy asked.

"You sure the falcon's dead?" McDermott asked.

Oh yeah, it was dead.

"I don't know, Andrew," Jonas said to Becky's dad. "You really shouldn't be driving."

Jonas told Randy to turn off the searchlights on the truck and drive it back to the ranch. Jonas and Becky were going to pile into her dad's pickup and go directly to the hospital.

"I'll follow you there," Randy said. What happened if Mr. McDermott's truck broke down again, he explained.

"It didn't break down," Becky said. "He already told you that. Geez, Randy."

Randy looked at Becky and let her rude demeanor go. She'd been worried about her dad. She broke into tears when they found him. She was emotional. "Heck, Becky. I'm sorry."

Randy was surprised to find Walking Eagle McDermott so easily, sitting on the ground, singing aloud along with that weird church song. At first, he thought the old man was drunk, but he didn't smell liquor, and he walked back to the truck fine. He was wincing, though, holding his hand and squeezing it to his body.

"Hey, I'm fine. I wasn't meant to be trampled by elk or eaten by lions. God had a precise way for me to be found. Unbelievable, Randy. Unbelievable."

Randy looked over at Oscar. Oscar looked up at him, more proud of himself than ever.

Becky's plan to find the truck with the music didn't work, but they found it parked on the side of the road anyway. The speakers weren't hooked up correctly, she said. She held the phone up and played the song off the phone's speaker. Walking Eagle had accidentally turned off the sound on the phone.

After a few verses of "Be still my soul," they heard Walking Eagle singing along. Oscar ran right to him, barking into the fog. Randy carefully followed, glad Oscar was barking, and the old man was singing. The fog blanketed everything just twenty feet from the truck. Becky followed right behind him. At one point he had to grab her hand. She let him. After she tripped.

The two of them ended up helping Walking Eagle get back to his truck. Jonas kept shouting from the road to lead them back. Oscar barked like he knew what he was doing.

Walking Eagle was laughing when they got to him, and all the way back. He kept laughing about how God had a sense of humor. Neither Randy nor Becky thought the rescue was funny. Not in any way.

Randy was surprised at how difficult it was to return to the road. The fog hung thick in the air. Oscar led them, running back and forth, with Jonas hollering in the invisible mist. They couldn't keep up with Oscar and would have to stop every time he ran too far. Randy kept calling him back.

Randy liked Walking Eagle. He liked his daughter, too. She was rude but cute. She had an attitude, but it was because she was determined. He found that attractive in a girl.

The plus? His dog had found her dad.

Back at the trucks, Becky dropped to her knees. She hugged Oscar and let him lick at her tears. When Randy reached to help her get back up, she let him.

He said, "How crazy was that, huh?"

She punched him in the shoulder, hugged his dog again, and then looked him right in the eyes and said, "Thanks, Randy."

No way he wasn't going to follow them to the hospital.

Light washes over each species as they enter heaven, a flow by the millions each day, popping into this wondrous place together, a slow exploding array of holy bodies. Some appear on the ground next to welcoming trees and springs. Those in the seas arrive with bubbling joy between plants, rocks, and sand. Arrivals date back millions and millions of years. Winged ancestors group around birds of every species, genus, and tribe, gathering together in the air. The same takes place for horses on the plains, bears in the mountains, and salmon in the water. Light reflects everywhere.

Amid the galloping, sauntering, hopping, and weaving betwixt and between, none are trampled, bumped, or elbowed, wrapped instead in a celestial display of ecstasy. You could say one can get used to the whelming welcome hoards, but no one says that.

The space to receive the increasing numbers grows with each entrance, extending the already vast heaven into multi-dimensions, flowing terrains, and stepped atmospheres. The shifting size of heaven's shape, always stretching in an understandable necessity, seems preposterous. Imagine a place with no limits. Every creature and plant acquires its habitat and gifted abundance custom-made.

Humans roam and abide among every species. How else would they live there? Fingers touch every class and order of being, with time to nurture and be nurtured, with plenty of room to spare for quiet walks and unbothered pondering.

Songs arise from bird lungs, expelled in cascades of concert trilled tunes with each feathered sway and dart in the air, often matching the movement of life on the land and waters below. No being competes, dominates, or is oppressed. Food hangs and falls from trees, bush, and vine into waiting arms, paws, and jaws. The same takes place in the air and in the seas.

No one is eaten anymore.

Chapter Six

CONSEQUENCES

*Holy obedience confounds all bodily and fleshly desires and keeps the
body mortified to the obedience of the spirit and to the obedience of
one's brother and makes a man subject to all the men of this world
and not to men alone, but also to all beasts and wild animals, so that
they may do with him whatsoever they will, in so far as it may be
granted to them from above by the Lord.*

—FROM THOMAS OF CELANO'S, "SECOND LIFE,"
WHERE HE RECORDED ST. FRANCIS OF ASSISI'S,
"SALUTATION OF THE VIRTUES" A.D. 1247

WORN OUT

HAIR, THE BEAR, DRAGGED his left leg. It wasn't working properly. He could
feel the ground against his paw as it lagged behind the rest of his body. He
couldn't make the leg operate.

The damage to his left side was mainly on the rear part, but he could
feel a tingling in his left arm, too. He had fallen several times as he worked
hard to get to his den. Hair hadn't been back to the cave since he'd left it on
the first spring thaw. He decided to go there now to see if he could rest and
get better.

Hair had eaten some meat stashed away by another animal a few days
earlier. The food was infected with fatal contaminations. Hair never had a
problem eating anything before today because contaminated food didn't
make much difference. An old bear now, though, Hair's ability to fend off
diseases had slowed down along with everything else. The winter naps increasingly took quite a toll.

Before his body exhibited paralysis on his left side, Hair was foraging
for some early growth on small bushes when he spied a group of hunters
and dogs traveling on a trail, carrying what looked like a dead lion. Its head

looked odd, the jaws propped open with a stick, bouncing loosely on the back end of a pole.

Hair avoided hunters. He had spent quite a bit of time a few years ago going through their trashcans, where many of them lived, just a day's walk from here. They had captured and transported him twice, and he didn't like the experience. So, he stayed away from them.

The found cache of contaminated food allowed him to stay away from the humans, but to unfortunate consequences. He watched the hunters leave with the lion, then wander further into the mountains. Traveling up-hill, though, proved more difficult than he could remember. Rather quickly, his body went through several stages of deterioration — first fever and then spasms along his back. The latest was his left leg going completely limp. He gave up his mountain climb and shifted to head to his hovel hidden in an upper ravine.

Finally, he drew near his den, deep into the forest, just below the giant mountain, Pikes Peak. He stood on his three good limbs, wavering and feverish, focusing his blurry eyes on the den's entrance. Maybe a few days' rest, he figured, though he didn't measure time in days. Bears aren't good at science, in either measurements or medicine. He needed to be alone and get his leg and left side working again.

By the time he got into his den, he was exhausted. He had squeezed, with difficulty, into the opening. His head wouldn't stop wagging to his left, and he fell with a blubbery thud into the spot where he had spent the winter.

Sleep came quickly.

In an hour or so, he was convulsing.

By morning, Hair was dead.

The doctor, Nelsen Virkman, repeated the conversation he'd had with Walking Eagle. The hospital used the very sick Indian's legal name, Andrew McDermott. The insurance paperwork insisted upon it. It was nothing rac-ist, the doctor insisted, though he wasn't quite sure about that. Dr. Virkman talked to the man's wife and daughter. The news wasn't good.

"He's always been in excellent health," Rachel McDermott said about her husband.

Becky sat holding her mother's hand, staring into her lap. Her dad needed quadruple bypass heart surgery. The explanation of what that meant was all too clear. She had sat in her school's biology class just a few months ago studying the various parts of the heart. The graphic and now frightening picture of what was going to happen to her dad hung in her thoughts.

Rachel ran through with the doctor her husband's recent bouts of indigestion. Some Walking Eagle had mentioned. The others she reported as her calculations. Lately, his increased need for sleep had worried her. She wondered out loud if she should have seen this coming.

"Well, let's say you did have some idea about how serious these things might have been, Mrs. McDermott," the doctor said. "Indigestion and sleepiness aren't clear warning signs of a serious heart issue. What impact on your husband would your concerns have had?"

Becky giggled and cried at the same time. "You would have told him to eat slower," Becky said to her mother.

"Yeah," Rachel said, nodding. She squeezed her daughter's hand.

They thanked the doctor and went to see their husband and father. He was being prepped for emergency surgery. They had just a few minutes to see him.

Randy sat on the back step of the house he was repairing. It stood not far from the center of Castle Rock. Oscar sat next to him, staring out at the back yard which he had successfully turned into a fenced lot of dirt. Grass clumps that Randy's father expected to morph into a carpet of grass were long gone.

Randy looked at his dog, who gave him a practiced glance of, "Yeah, I see you admiring me," and thought about Becky's family. Randy never imagined life without a father. He found out at the hospital that Mr. Mc-Dermott's chances weren't great after this kind of heart surgery. The surgery was commonplace, but Walking Eagle's condition was not.

Randy, his uncle Jonas, and the McDermott family chatted in the hospital room with Walking Eagle. They exchanged snippets about dead lions and hunting dog tracks. Walking Eagle pieced together Randy's visit and the dead lion near the den. Randy's dogs had been the ones on the Clayhall Ranch. Randy explained that he'd only fired a warning shot that morning. Upon further discussion, he found out his careened shot off a rock matched the skull location and subsequent death of the male mountain lion Walking Eagle knew.

Appalled by the news, Randy crossed his arms above his head in horror. Mr. McDermott was just doing his job, trying to identify the culprit who indiscriminately bushwhacked a lion and then abandoned the kill. In pursuit of the trespasser, Walking Eagle succumbed to a near-fatal heart attack.

Randy's face went pale, and then he fainted, crumpling into his father's arms. After waking him with smelling salts, the doctor told Randy that he probably saved McDermott's life. If Walking Eagle hadn't gone hiking and exacerbated his heart activity, he may have simply died in his sleep one night.

The kind words were no consolation to Randy. He told everyone he was sorry and then left, but not before Mr. McDermott shook his hand and thanked him and Oscar for finding him. Randy couldn't look at Becky.

He didn't throw up until he got home.

"You're the real hero," he said to Oscar on their back porch. Randy's cell phone was in his shirt pocket. His uncle said he would call when Mr. McDermott was out of surgery.

Oscar lifted his head, portraying the pose of a canine savior of lost men, and yawned. He wondered if he and Randy were going to sleep out here together tonight.

Hair opened his eyes and rolled his head toward what he thought was the opening of his den. A brilliant light shone at his feet. He looked down at his left leg and wiggled his foot. It felt just fine.

He then rolled his entire body up to a sitting position and looked up. The top of the den had disappeared. He was no longer in his cave. All around him was darkness, save for the sunbeam shining right in front of him.

Hair didn't feel sleepy, and his body wiggled as he rocked his bottom to the left and then to the right several times to be sure all his parts were working. He snuffed the air, and it smelled sweet and wet, tickling his nose.

The darkness behind him emitted gurgling, bubbly noises. Hair scratched the ground to silence the noises. They continued with louder groans and barks. Hair sat still for a moment, wondering at the strange calls trying to get his attention. He shook his head and roared for them to be quiet.

Which they immediately did.

The ground felt cushy under his feet and front paws as he fell forward onto all fours, directed to the oddly shiny rays in front of him. He heard a whistling sound in the light, and he stretched his neck, so his head just reached the light, and tipped his ears to catch the source of the sound. The darkness in front of him slowly faded away to a daytime scene, similar to his mountain home. Yet, so much more — like it would be on its best day.

A singsong whistle calling him drew him further into a picturesque environment. Voices amid the whistling joined familiar forest sounds of leaves rustling, water nearby, and insects clicking. He walked on all fours into the light, blinking away the previous darkness, and took in a shocking sight.

Several bears sat on rocks, staring toward him. He stepped further forward, curious and cautious. Bears of all sizes, shapes, and colors took form. They exhibited no aggression or fear at his arrival. He thought he'd interrupted them but sensed that they were waiting for him. He couldn't tell which.

To his right, a stream ran through the rocks, down a winding ridge, straight into the horizon, a magnificent array of clouds and sky. The area where he stood banked in a large ledge of space against a lush mountainside. Plants, trees, brush, and grass grew everywhere.

A bear stood up, paddled his paws in the air, and then sat right back down. He was big. Hair's eyebrows creased into surprise. That bear looked a lot like his father. Another bear moved, a female. She leaned up against the large bear and patted the ground in front of her. Hair took stilted steps toward them. He recognized her, too. Was that his mother?

He looked at the other bears, and they began pounding the ground, making more whistling sounds and grunting at him.

Hair turned — no den back there, just more lovely, lush landscape. He ran back a few steps to be sure. The bears went quiet. He turned back to them. They remained silent, eyes studying him, watching what he would do.

Hesitant but stepping slowly, Hair walked to them, confused about getting to this place. The two bears, which he thought could be his mother and father, began to walk to him, also on all fours, grunting gently. A couple of squirrels ran by him from behind, startling him. They skidded to the rocks, jumped onto his father's shoulders, and ran around his back, chasing each other. Hair sat back and watched the squirrels hop away and through the crowd.

Then he realized that many weren't bears at all. One looked like a wild boar, and another was a raccoon sitting in the arms of a man.

Hair felt weak in his joints, and he cocked his head sideways to see if the picture changed. It did. There were more and many different animals.

His mother walked to him without hesitation. She crawled into his lap and rested her head next to his. Hair's father stood up and started spinning in circles. The whistling started up again, and Hair realized it was coming from the raccoon and the man.

Hair wrapped his arms around his mother and squeezed. Her familiar breath filled his nose. She rubbed his shoulders and gripped him closely. They frolicked on the ground, rolling like a giant ball, landing against his spinning father, who fell and joined them as they hugged together. All the while, the crowd grunted, whistled, and stamped the ground.

Snarl and Tuft subdued, then dispatched, an injured elk just before dawn.

Snarl smelled elk when the fog lifted. Tuft scratched at prints in the dirt, a meandering set of elk hooves, soon after they walked into the valley. Snarl bumped Tuft's hip to follow him. The tracks showed the elk limped on three legs. Together, they stopped and spied the animal ahead in a well-hidden grove near the lower part of the valley. It sat, oddly, in a sitting position. They found him in just a few minutes and circled to the right between bushes and trees outside the view of the sitting elk.

Tuft knew what Snarl wanted. She crept directly toward the elk coming into its left side periphery, spooking it at the last second to stand up and defend itself. Snarl was upon the elk's throat from behind before the elk could position an effective defense. It had a damaged rear leg and boldly bleated at them but was no match for the two lions.

They ate until full and buried the rest.

The hike back to their den took quite a while. Tuft kept retracing their way. When they reached the rise just before hitting the ridge to their lair, she backtracked almost to the buried cache. Snarl watched in amazement. When she returned, she trotted single-minded, unwavering, back to the den.

She squealed again during an extra-long yawn, just as they were getting to sleep. It didn't bother Snarl this time. He licked her face as she closed her eyes and scooted up close to him. His stomach full, he watched the sunlight erase the dawn's haze, brightening the entrance to their den. The light exaggerated the darkness inside. Snarl was soon asleep.

Snort, a young elk with already poor prospects on two significant fronts — assembling his herd and the comfort of brother elk to boost predatory defense — accidentally trapped his rear leg in a jumble of rocks while on a dead run. He had no brother elk to mount a defensive front. They'd run ahead after the herd. Snort had no cows to form his own herd. Things did not look good.

The foot stuck because he was in a hurry. He'd misread the hidden danger beneath a pile of leaves. Snort had become more jittery with each passing day, and this mistake would be catastrophic.

A bit of good news saved him from hunting lions the day before. Snort hobbled for safety into a forest edge of the valley when two buck elk raced by at top speed. Two lions ran full strides right behind them. Snort stood still, watching as they disappeared from view.

The damage to his foot was more than Snort first imagined. His leg had cracked just above the ankle, but he had run on it anyway. Panicked, trying pitifully to keep up with the migrating herd on only three good legs, Snort's progress slowed. A full day passed, and he stopped here after he'd seen the lions. The herd was long gone. The exhaustion of travel and pressure on his leg eventually had shattered the bone completely. He stood on three legs, unable to even hop.

Snort spent the night standing on three legs, hidden somewhat in the trees and brush. His good back leg began shaking uncontrollably just before dawn, deteriorated after carrying all his weight. He sat, or rather, fell back like a calf, his broken leg splayed sideways. His breaths came in quick, choppy heaves. Snort stared into the valley from his hiding spot, waiting for help or some other good luck.

As time passed, animals wandered by, and birds flew around him, unconcerned over his presence. A pair of rabbits played nearby. Snort watched the increasing activity, surprised that he'd never seen so many living things this close before. They were carefree, and he enjoyed the scenes around him.

He saw, too late, a lion stalking him. He jumped up on his three good legs when it growled. Snort bugled out his best warrior cry. When he flung his head at a second lion who jumped against his side, he caught a glimpse of teeth gripping at his neck, and all went black.

Howl crawled out of the coyote family den and jogged almost a mile up to the craggy outcrop rock where he would sit and awaken the world. Enjoying his new morning exercise, Howl earned this benefit afforded to the ruling dog in the pack. He took over the clan with immediate success and took advantage of all the perks. He especially liked the morning and evening perches where he would survey the coyote territory while the rest of the pack remained safely near the den.

The sun was shining. Howl laid out on the warm rock and looked over the canyon to his right and then the prairie to his left. His post on the rock sat high above both.

A cloud covered the sun for a moment, revealing a single opening where a ray shone a spot just ahead. The beam of white, highlighting floating particles and flitting insects, hovered and then moved toward him.

He was breathing in the cool mountain air and letting out his warm breath in a gentle rhythm. Howl watched the sun's ray sidle up to a spot on the rock in front of him.

The coyote felt inspired, knew that even the sky recognized his importance, and it moved him. He stood up and howled at the beam of light, sensing that he should acknowledge its presence. He felt the light talk to him and saw a face in the light asking him to speak.

Howl spoke grandly.

Red, the fox, watched a beam of light slowly peek out of the sky and land to the right of a coyote who stood high on a rock, howling into the morning sun. Inside the bright shaft of light, the fox spotted a man floating in the beam. Red stretched his neck forward to sharpen his eyes.

The man resembled the fellow who brought him those gifts of eggs. Red quietly pranced, his feet barely touching the ground, to get closer to the man in the light. Yes, that's him. Again!

Both the coyote and the man looked upward into the source of the white stream which encased the man. Neither the man nor the coyote noticed Red.

That man has an egg with him, Red saw. He wasn't singing, but his right hand tightly closed around something white. With a running start, he could jump and get it. He had to be quick and not startle the coyote.

Red pranced faster and faster, closer and closer. The coyote howled and did not sense Red trotting from behind.

The fox raced up the rock and leaped to the right side of the crooning coyote. Red saw that the coyote's eyes were closed in a trance as he dove. Red flew into the light where the man floated in midair. The fox snapped at the man's fist, and glanced at the same facial expression on the fellow in the field just hours ago.

Red's dive ended gracefully, landing him without harm below the rock. He looked back, and the man was gone. The light had disappeared. The coyote still looked upward but had stopped howling. Red felt for the egg with his tongue, which he imagined was resting behind his teeth, but it wasn't there.

The coyote looked behind where he stood, probably only now recognizing that something had burst from behind him. Red took off, shaken at his bold move so close to two dangerous enemies. He ran, disappointed in missing the egg, and wondered if there was any light or man after all.

The coyote spun in circles, looking for the light and the thing that flew by him. Red skittered further and further from the coyote, unseen, a bit unnerved, and somehow tasting an egg where no egg had been nabbed.

Walking Eagle held the hands of both his wife and his daughter. He lay flat on his back, strapped to a gurney pausing in the hall before heading to surgery. Becky kindly accommodated him, starting the prayer he had asked them to pray together. She pleaded that the Spirit of God be with the doctor and those helping him.

"Because dad will not be just asleep," she said. "He will be looking for the light. He wants to be with you, face to face, and we're not ready for that to happen. Not just yet."

"Amen," Rachel chimed in. "Please bring him back to us."

Walking Eagle had trouble speaking because his daughter prayed for precisely what he was thinking. Look for white light, and then call out for Jesus. All he said to his daughter was, "Wow."

The prayer was specific. Becky and her mother were not ready for Walking Eagle to go.

The nurse turned on the IV drip anesthetic. "It's time," she said.

Walking Eagle could not move his lips before the gurney began rolling away. He tried to smile at his wife and daughter as he left, but his face had gone slack. His eyes still worked fine, and he saw them blowing him kisses.

Walking Eagle watched ceiling tiles sliding by. Quietly, yet quickly, the beige hall turned into a sparsely clouded night sky. He felt himself lifted upright, floating in the air in a standing position. He gripped at the gurney where he had been laying down and held onto a fistful of sheet. How can I be standing on air, he asked?

In front of him sat a coyote, standing on a rock, looking to the sky, then directly at Walking Eagle, floating in the air. Walking Eagle looked up and saw a gleaming white entrance just above him.

"Hello," he said, looking back to the coyote. "I'm getting my heart fixed, but it might not work." The coyote rocked his body in place, breathing through his open mouth, and stared at Walking Eagle.

"I don't suppose you can hear me," McDermott said.

The coyote lifted his head and howled into the air.

McDermott peered upward too, squinting into the light where the coyote aimed his howl. Something bit at his left hand; the one Walking Eagle still gripped at his bedsheet. He saw the top of a fox flying through the beam of light. It startled him, and the light cleared in an instant. After blinking away the scene, Walking Eagle looked around, and he was lying flat, completely wrapped in a crispy set of sheets, not floating and not standing in a beam of light.

"Oh my," he said. His heart hurt, and he closed his eyes.

"I was ready, Lord," he mouthed, understanding that he wasn't going into the light. Not just yet. He fell asleep.

Walking Eagle woke up moments later, in his mind. It had been almost six hours. Becky and Rachel were standing at his right, touching his arm.

"Dad," Becky said.

He looked at her, then over at Rachel.

"How are you feeling," Rachel asked.

Their worried faces looked as grim as the moment when he took off for the operation. He smiled at them and then giggled a bit before saying, "I had to come back. Not much time to look for Jesus. After the coyote sang to me, that crazy fox jumped right at me. The same one, I think. He interrupted me, sent me back, I guess before I could even get directions."

Rachel patted his arm while Becky breathed out, relieved that her father's hallucinations were still as active as ever.

"Thank you, Jesus," she whispered.

Walking Eagle smiled at her.

REPRIEVE

Snarl sat high on the rock surrounded by brush that looked over the entrance to Tuft's den. His and Tuft's den. The wedge of the valley below looked calm. The cache of elk remained. They would eat again today. Water still gurgled down the warm rocks across the canon.

Tuft exited the den, yawned, and squealed out.

Snarl stood, looking down at her. Tuft turned to see him and then took off, jogging in the direction of the rock-fed stream.

He watched Tuft go. She knew Snarl's eyes were on her. Tuft did not hesitate, assured that he could see her. She knew where to go.

Snarl sat to wait for her.

His life now would be lived in this canyon, he considered. As a lion considers the future, that is. A lion's past is not a prologue as an animal ponders things. It is as much present to him as the present, which is also how the future takes place.

Snarl waited for Tuft to return and for her to lay down next to him. He made no plans for food beyond what was at hand. The den already was his home, and food would be available, just as it always was.

He did not yet know much about men. Tuft did not know about them either. They also did not realize that they lived on a ranch owned by a man. When they found out about humans, what they would do then was not on their minds.

Bears and humans rested along a beach. Their task for the last few hours had been to make a long and lovely perching space for the creatures who swam or surfed in from the waters. Since no half or empty shell lay about — because all shells still held their inhabitants in the divine arenas of heaven — the sunning of aquatic crustaceans was as much a vision to behold as it was a fastidious function of being an exoskeleton being.

The bears dragged and pushed and rolled the boulders that formed the beginnings of a wall. The humans wedged wood chunks, non-decaying timbers of course (since decay is no longer), into the spaces between the boulders.

Everyone munched on vegetation from the bushes near the waters. The wood supplies fell like gifts from branches willingly dropped by the semi-sentient trees that grew behind the bush.

As described in an earlier life, Hardwoods offered their growth, complete with the beauty of gnarls and barked bits. The range of woods for construction, produced by willing forest growth, is used for every imaginable purpose.

Harvests of vegetation both in and outside of imaginations supply the food and medicine for creation. Medicine is for therapeutic use rather than remedy or medication. There is nothing here to rectify, fix, or repair. Medicine meets needs throughout the process of life like fruit and the misty air.

Woods, fibers, roots, and flowers weave into every living activity. Consequently, when an array of shellfish visits the land population, the woods among the boulders display grainy splendor against smooth shellfish surfaces, accentuating their saturated colors. The presentation is endlessly stunning to behold. The boulders sparkle and finish off the fabulous picture of the ocean's entertainment.

All this takes place to everyone's delight. But especially to the bears and humans.

Hair joined in the task. He liked to dip and dive into the waters between each journey bringing the men and women boulders to fashion a stage for the ocean creatures.

He has been learning to dance, by the way.

TALK

Becky sat on the front door stoop of Randy's house in Castle Rock. He sat next to her, about a foot between them. She had been talking for several minutes while Randy listened. As she spoke, moving her hands and making quite a commotion with distracting body movements that highlighted her different emotions, Randy decided he had better take stalk of the entirely one-way conversation. She was lovely to watch, but he should take in the meaning of her words as much as her physical presence.

To assess the string of things Becky had been talking about, he ticked off in his head her "points," as she called them. He'd never spoken with a girl before, he realized. Not like this.

There were five points so far. That is five points subsequent to three questions — none of which Randy answered adequately.

"Do you have a girlfriend?"

Before answering that question, Becky said she wanted to "point out" that she was only 17, going on 18, and that Randy was a grown man of 19.

"Girlfriend" was not her first question. It was the latest one and the spark that moved him to review everything she had said since she arrived. Her first question was whether he had come to terms with the "overwhelming awfulness" of her father's heart attack, "because neither she nor her mother held it against him."

He was not "over" the awfulness. He didn't say that out loud. Instead, he stared at his shoes. Blood rushed to his head, and he sat frozen in place. He did not want to cry. Becky touched him on the arm and said, "Of course not." She explained she shouldn't have asked that question and then went on to great detail, assuring Randy that it would take him time to come to terms with something that was not his fault.

"It may, in 'point' of fact, have saved my dad's life."

Becky's second question had to do with how much she liked his dog. Did Randy remember meeting Becky five years earlier at the veterinarian's animal hospital where her mother worked? At that question, Randy looked at her face, very surprised. He was pretty sure he had not met her before yesterday.

"I was only 11 at the time, but I certainly remember you," she explained. After incredible detail about a fifteen-minute visit Randy made to the vet. He needed shots for his brand-new puppy, whom he had yet to name. The vet visit memory came back in 3-D color with sounds and smells.

"Oh, yes," he said while staring at her face. Yes was not a correct answer because Randy didn't remember her. He remembered the vet and not having named Oscar. He did not recognize her face. Becky had a lovely face, though.

Randy looked back at his shoes.

"I want to point out that I suggested that you needed to name your dog," Becky said.

Randy looked back at Becky with a visible start, unsure how to factor in this girl's memory to his recollections. He could not remember how he came up with Oscar's name.

"I was holding my Oscar the Grouch doll." Becky was entirely sure about that.

"I pointedly told you that Oscar isn't really a bad person. When you called to Oscar in the truck last night, I was really pleased."

Oscar walked over and sat down between the two. His front paws gripped the edge of the first step. He looked out into the front yard. Whether on the front or back porch Oscar enjoyed sitting next to Randy.

That's when Becky asked Randy if he had a girlfriend and made her final point that she was 17 years old, going on 18, recognizing that he was a grown-up 19.

"Going on 20," Randy then added.

It was time he made a point.

A NOD AND SHRUG

Walking Eagle rocked quietly in one of the handmade Amish glider chairs that Jonas lined up on his patio, facing out to the valley at the east end of the ranch. He had thanked Jonas so many times for the many kindnesses over the past three months that Jonas finally asked him to, "Cut it out."

A small herd of deer had been camping out under a stand of pines a few hundred yards from the house.

"I think they feel safe out there," Jonas said. For the umpteenth time to Walking Eagle, he described how the deer arrived right about the time of his heart attack. "I think it's you. They just won't go away."

"Jeez, Jonas," the Indian said.

A few minutes ago, Randy and his dog had taken off, driving in Randy's truck to make the afternoon's rounds. Randy had picked up Walking Eagle's duties after agreeing to work for his uncle.

"I think it was my daughter who talked him into it," Walking Eagle said.

"He's smitten," Jonas said.

"Doggone right," said Walking Eagle, who wasn't sure how he felt about that.

Pikes Beak hovered like a Humming Bird in front of his nest, something falcons don't usually know how to do. Floating in one place was a new talent he'd acquired, along with this amazing nest. He looked about and spied innumerable nesting places. On his flight here he'd seen eagles, herons, and other flying creatures he hadn't imagined existed. Their housing ranged from large caves in hillsides to the tiniest of hovelled openings in massive trees.

Falcons, like most animals, don't have mathematical skills. Pikes Beak knew only that the vastness of space for winged creatures was beyond anything he'd seen before.

The hawk he'd met that first day, or whatever time ago that was, flew him to this place, his new home. The home delighted Pikes Beak. So many colors and mix of living leaves, fingered branches cupped for catching water, and warm, soothing light everywhere.

The many-faceted abode, complete with resting areas, perches, and even a ledge for eating the fruits and seeds and other snacks he had already tasted was built by grasshoppers, ants, small birds, and a snake with legs.

After a lengthy winged tour, interspersed with lovely landings in all the places he would inhabit, he noticed a recurring familiarity in the tiny insects. He looked closely at the birds guiding him on the tour, and the small and even large animals still busy on his home's construction. All of them were beings that Pikes Beak had eaten in his earthly life. Except for the snake, who looked nothing like the meal Pikes Beak had gulped down only a few weeks ago. The snake he remembered had no legs. He'd only eaten one snake in his life. And there he was, wandering around, giving ants burdened with bits of building materials rides to and fro.

All these former sources of food in his earlier life were here when he showed up. They were even giddy with excitement at his arrival, each one buzzing around him, crawling over his feet, and singing, sort of, in a strange act of caressing and care.

Another amazement struck him. He had no desire to eat any of them. He could see the same in their eyes. Every living thing that Pikes Beak had eaten crossed his path in this wonderful world. They were alive again. The same was true for each of them. Anything anyone had eaten was now part of a big, connected family.

Pikes Beak didn't understand what happened here, but that wasn't part of his makeup anyway. He didn't figure stuff out. It just immediately made sense to him, or it didn't, and he responded in kind. No fears. No worries. No paranoia. Just a constant, guiding sound suggesting what he should do next, followed by his eager cooperation.

The sound that guided him comforted him, too. He knew it from his previous life, the voice of a wise falcon. No, it was from more than a falcon. A caretaker. A being that prompted the light he was seeing, and the building of the house these others were making for him. This being knew him, and everyone else.

Pikes Beak was gloriously happy. Even delirious at times. He began his new life immediately, with intense engagement. A power surged through him, steady, strong, and careful too. He showed off his joy to anyone who looked his way, singing to both people and animals, even kissing them when it seemed appropriate.

Oh, and the berries.

Unbelievable, every single time.

Very soon, Pikes Beak met the creature behind the sound. The sound called to him, and Pikes Beak left to find him, far away from his home. He could see him waving all the way there. His eyes had become sharp, telescopic at distances that would amaze any falcon.

Pikes Beak arrived at an open space where a man stood. He was the fellow behind the sound and all the waving. He stood in a low lush garden arena. Pikes Beak hung in the air, wings spread, in front of the man, a golden smiling creature. After holding and touching Pikes Beak, caressing his wings and head, the man introduced the falcon to more humans. He began to hear their voices, and was able to understand them. Birds flew everywhere, landing on outstretched hands.

The sound of voices was no longer just in his head, but all around him.

Pikes Beak didn't want to leave. The sound asked him, speaking in his mind most clearly this time, if he was pleased with the home he had built for him. The falcon's heart yearned to go back to his nest. The golden man told him he would come to see him and spend time there with him and his family of creatures.

The falcon nodded, filled with expectation and longing. Then the man looked down at the ground in front of him.

Pikes Beak did too, and saw some animals waving at him. He flew down, realizing he was being asked to pick them up. An entire family of chipmunks began touching his feathers and chirping at him. He understood what their chirps meant.

Pikes Beak was to carry them off to see some turtles they knew at a pond on his way back home. How did he know that's where they were headed? The golden man arranged the whole thing, and soon the chipmunks were communicating with him — with glances, pointing, and sounds that had meaning.

After holding his wings outstretched for the chipmunks, Pikes Beak was able to get one of the other human's attention. He didn't know how that worked. The human walked over and helped lift one of the stragglers on board, purring with the rest of his family on the falcon's wings.

Pikes Beak then flew into the air, hinting to his passengers when to lean toward or back, left or right. He weaved, dove, and swooped for effect. The falcon knew he was going to be really good at giving exciting rides.

Prance's fawn spotted two coyotes, and pointed them out to her mother. She had grown up quickly.

One fawn, and an injured buck who hung around with them, had both been taken down by coyotes over the last few months. Another wandering fawn had been quickly and silently captured by a lion on their migrant move. They were traveling in the evening, because there was no moon at that time. Moonless nights were the times that scared the deer the most.

Their herd losses, however, were not enough to move them away from their new nightly spot near a human nesting area. Only when they were out and about, making their daily walks up into the canyon did real danger come to them.

The coyote hid on the ridge where they would be traveling soon. The fawn didn't put that together, yet, but Prance did. She looked at Sharp Eyes. He'd spied them, too.

This meant they were probably going to change their grazing paths. Their patterns had been figured out. Prance would have to decide whether to follow Sharp Eyes, or move on. She still couldn't decide.

That's the problem with danger, she thought to herself. It was more important to be bunched up with a herd than off by herself. She knew then that she would stay with Sharp Eyes. Her best option remained with him. She pushed away the nagging urge to run, sensing another voice telling her it was right to remain with the others. She nudged her fawn under her front legs. The little one was little no more, almost fully grown. She licked her daughter's face, and turned to Sharp Eyes, letting him know he was still in charge.

This season's antlers now grown quite large swayed as the buck nodded his head up and down, over and over. He was pleased with her. The larger their herd, the better. Especially with this special deer in their company.

Tuft carried at least one kitten in her womb. She didn't know how many she might have. She could feel her teats extending already, though they did not show. Memory of suckling her mother explained everything to her.

Her fur had filled in, weight put on, and her strength had reached a full, steady coursing in her muscles. She had never felt this good before, and walked with a new confidence.

Snarl looked often at Tuft, studying her body and how it seemed to change daily. He had no idea about any kittens growing inside her.

They were used to each other, lightly bumping sides as they hiked, rubbing each other's heads, licking away any blood or pieces of food off their faces and paws and legs.

They walked across a flat space, and watched a truck coming toward them. Snarl stopped, then walked across the truck's path. He watched the truck slow down. The machine, which they didn't know wasn't alive, followed the same schedule every day. It remained safely on its path, which Snarl figured out must have been formed by those odd black circular feet.

The boy, or man, or whatever a lion thinks about a human, hung one arm out of the dark green beast. With his other arm he held a piece of the truck to his face. Or, something like that. Camera phones don't resemble anything in the wild. The daily scene of the truck never ceased to interest Snarl. It smelled bad, like a felled tree on fire. He and Tuft needed to study it more, and yet stay clear of it.

Satisfied for the moment, Snarl walked on with Tuft at his side. He listened for any guidance from the voice he heard more and more each day in his head. The voice could convey many things, including a convincing shrug of dismissal. The green animal, housing that human, was of no evil consequence to him.

Tuft, concerned about the encounter, a regular event, looked to Snarl for an assessment. Snarl copied the shrug he heard in his head, dismissed the beast and its inhabitant as an enemy, and the two of them turned away headed for their den.